Next Door Knight

Dedication

For my sister Joanne,
Here's to milestones: thirty-first book for me, milestone birthday for you.
Love you, Sis.

Chapter One

KERRY WILLIAMS WANTED slink to her bedroom, jump into bed, pull the covers over her head, and hide from the world for the next two months. Unfortunately, life didn't work out that way, so she had to suck it up and play the cards she'd been dealt.

The only good thing? Her new house was a major step up on what she'd been living in only a few weeks ago. Of course, if she didn't find her dog and get her ass to her new job, she'd be back to living in a one-bedroom apartment in the seedy part of San Antonio.

"Kerry, honey, I'm thirsty. Can you get me a drink, please?" Her father's voice floated down the hallway to where she stood in the kitchen, looking at the empty backyard, where only ten minutes ago, her corgi, Willow, was running around, enjoying all the extra space she now had to play in.

Oh crap, why now? She needed to find Willow, but if she didn't pour Dad a tall glass of orange juice, he would attempt to get it himself and probably wind up flat on his face. Ambulances weren't cheap.

A glance at her watch and her blood pressure rose further. "Where the hell is this new caregiver? She was supposed to be here five minutes ago. Hopefully, she's just running late," Kerry said to the empty kitchen as she fixed her father his drink.

Dad was sitting in her favorite chair in the living room, his plaster-clad legs propped up on the cushion, the late afternoon sun highlighting the gray in his hair. His crutches leaned against the side of the chair, within easy reach for him to hobble over to the wheelchair residing in the corner of the room.

There was no way her father could've stayed with her in her former residence. Going up four flights of stairs to a one-bedroom apartment wasn't an option for a man with two broken legs.

"Here you go, Dad. A nice glass of juice for you."

"I'd prefer a cold beer," he grumbled, but he took the glass and drank down half the contents.

"You know what the doctor said. No alcohol while you're on painkillers and antibiotics."

"I know. I know. But it's hot, and there's nothing like a good beer to take away the heat of the day."

Kerry refrained from rolling her eyes. A shiver wracked her body as the air conditioner kicked in. Of course, Dad liked it set at sixty-eight degrees. Her ideal temperature was a balmy seventy-six. "You're sitting in a nice cold room; I think the juice will be sufficient for you."

Her dad chuckled and finished off his drink. "Don't you

need to be leaving for your job?"

"Yes, but I can't leave until the caregiver arrives, and Willow's disappeared from the backyard. She's never done this before. I need to go find her."

Her father waved a hand in the air. "Go. I don't need no babysitter. I can get around just fine."

Kerry closed her eyes and counted to ten in an attempt to not bite off her dad's head. "You have two broken legs, Dad. You can't get around easily."

Thank goodness Dad had good health insurance that covered a home-care service. No way could she afford an expense like that on top of her new mortgage payment.

"It's an unnecessary cost. I can just imagine the increase in my premium when I come to renew it."

Kerry would love the luxury of having health insurance. But until she passed the probation period in her new job, the benefits discussed in her interview were moot. "Just be glad you have it." She checked her watch again. "If she doesn't come soon, I'm going to have to call in and say I can't make it."

Damn, that was the last thing she wanted to do. She really liked her new job as manager of a hip restaurant on the Riverwalk. Just her luck it was all going to fall in a heap and she'd be out of a job and then she'd have to go back to living in a hovel of an apartment with no yard for Willow.

Willow.

Why did she have to choose today of all days to go on an

adventure?

Kerry rubbed her forehead, willing away the headache forming behind her eyes. "I need to go look for Willow, will you be okay, Dad?"

"I'll be fine, love." He reached out and squeezed her arm. "I appreciate you taking me in. I know it's inconvenient having me live with you."

She leaned down and bussed her dad on the cheek. "It's not an inconvenience. Besides, where else would you go? You and Mom looked after me. It's only fair I look after you."

He cleared his throat. "You're doing your mom proud, love."

A lump formed in her throat and she pushed down the tears threatening to overflow. "I hope she will be. I miss her."

"I miss her too." His eyes misted and he cleared his throat. "Now go find your dog so you can make it to work."

Another glance at her watch. The home nurse was now almost fifteen minutes late and Kerry had thirty-five minutes until she had to be at work. Hopefully, Willow hadn't wandered too far.

After firing off another text to the home-care agency employee, she grabbed the dog's leash from the hall table and stepped outside. Spring and summer in San Antonio had passed in a blink of an eye and still the sun beat down on her head, even though it was supposed to be fall. Maybe having the house temperature set like an ice block wasn't a bad idea after all.

With her heart in her mouth, she looked at the road, praying she wouldn't see Willow lying in the middle. Her breath whooshed out. All clear.

Which direction should Kerry go?

If I were a dog, where would I run?

Kerry still had no idea how the dog had escaped her backyard in the first place. There was a fence surrounding the whole property; access to the front yard was almost impossible. But dogs were wily creatures.

"Willow?" she called as she marched off down the street, her head turned to the side hoping to see her cute corgi's face staring at her from across the road or see her little brown butt wiggling from side to side as she strutted down the sidewalk.

Nothing. Not a single furry face or wiggly butt to be seen.

She bent to peer through the bushes bordering the front of a house just down from hers. Again a blank yard greeted her. She stood and grabbed her hair, twirling it around her finger, a stress habit she couldn't shake.

"Dammit, Willow where are you?" she muttered and turned around to head back home. Perhaps her dog would be sitting on the front porch when she got there. She pulled her phone from her pocket—had the agency responded to her text message?

Thunk.

She careened into something hard and soft, two contrasting sensations that meshed together well.

Stunned, it took her a few seconds to comprehend what she'd run in to. Kerry looked up and swallowed.

Standing before her was the sexiest man she'd seen in a long time, taller than her by about a foot. He had shaggy, dark brown hair that flopped over his forehead, covering one of his chocolate-brown eyes. Dressed in blue jeans and a T-shirt that hugged him in all the right places, he looked like he belonged in a magazine, not on the sidewalk of a quiet neighborhood in San Antonio. And, cradled in his big strong arms, was Willow, her tongue lolling out of the side of her mouth as she panted. A happy smile adorned her white doggy face, as though she'd found heaven and had no plans on leaving anytime soon.

Kerry couldn't really blame her dog. Those arms looked like they could take the weight of the world in them.

"Are you planning to stand here all day, mute?" The gravelly voice from the stranger rippled down her spine like a feather floating on the breeze. It immediately conjured up images of him whispering sweet nothings in her ear.

Whoa, hold up, girl. We're so not going there right now.

Yeah, yeah, the little voice in her head had tried to talk some sense into her on numerous occasions and she'd ignored it each time. But, heck, the stranger's voice did suit him perfectly. It sounded like he never used it much and only when he had something important to say.

At that moment, Willow let out a little bark. "Do you

happen to know whose dog this is?" he asked. "According to its collar, its name is Willow, but the number listed is disconnected."

Crap, she totally meant to get that updated.

"Willow's my dog. I was just looking for her."

"Here." He shoved Willow toward her, as if her dog stank like rotten trash, which Kerry knew wasn't possible as she'd given Willow a bath yesterday. "Your dog is found."

Kerry grabbed Willow before she crashed to the ground. What a jerk. Why rescue a lost dog when it was clear he can't stand to be around one?

"Thanks for finding her."

He grunted and swiveled, striding down the pavement toward the house next to hers, a limp marring his perfect stride. Willow let out a little whimper, as if she were sad to see her friend go.

Well, tough. Her fur baby had caused her enough stress, and if Kerry didn't get her butt home soon, she'd be out of a job.

"Come on, you. I don't know what you thought you were doing, but it's time to go home. You can keep your granddaddy out of trouble. Oh, shit."

The caregiver still hadn't turned up. And her phone remained ominously quiet with no responses to her texts.

In the two months she'd been living here, she hadn't had a chance to meet anyone that she could ask. Some of her dad's friends were busy at their weekly bowling game, and it was tournament week, so all hands on deck were needed. John, his former business partner, had retired to Georgetown and it would take him almost two hours to get here. She couldn't wait that long. Maybe she could ask Dad to call his new friend Eric and see if he could come over and sit with him for the evening.

If Eric could make it, her dad couldn't be left alone until he arrived. As a former construction worker, sitting still was an anomaly to Dad.

She looked to her neighbor's house then back at her own.

"Do you think he'd help out, Willow?"

Some people might think it crazy that she talked to her dog, but Willow was a therapy dog; over the months since she'd completed her training, she'd no doubt heard plenty of things.

Willow cocked her head and looked up, her brown eyes wide and her mouth seemed to stretch into a grin as she panted hot doggy breath in Kerry's face.

She screwed her nose up. "Well, I guess that's a yes."

Clipping Willow's leash around her sparkly pink collar, Kerry set her pet on the ground. There was no time to waste. She needed to knock on the door, ask the question, and pray to God he'd help her out and she'd be able to get to her job on time.

Taking a deep breath and pasting a smile on her face, she raised her fist and rapped her knuckles against the glass insert of the door. Only after she knocked did she think to check to see if he had a doorbell.

She spied the white circle nestled in a black rectangle on the doorframe.

Damn, there it was.

"Would it be rude if I pressed the doorbell after I just knocked on the door?" she asked her furry friend.

"Yes, it would." His voice sent shivers tiptoeing down her spine, again. Man, he needed to come with a warning—loner with deep, husky voice guaranteed to set her insides on fire, at her service.

Kerry bit back a snort of laughter. Knocking on this man's door was a complete mistake.

"Look, are you going to stand there and say nothing?"

She straightened her spine. "There's no need to be rude about it."

Yeah, now he's really going to help me.

Shit, this day was going from bad to worse to nightmarish. Life would've been so much easier if her father hadn't thought he was twenty again and could ski down a black diamond run.

THE LAST THING Caleb Bradshaw needed or wanted was this woman standing on his porch. He should've ignored the knock when he'd heard it. And continued to ignore it when he looked through the peephole and spied who was standing on his porch.

Hanging around people hadn't been high on his list of priorities since he'd finally extricated himself from his former girlfriend's clutches and his roommate had moved out.

"Did you need something? I gave you your dog back," he snapped.

Caleb willed himself to continue ignoring the furry creature panting quietly beside her owner. It brought back too many memories. Ones he struggled to deal with day after day. It hurt too much.

"I know this is a bit unusual, considering we don't know each other, but I'm in a desperate situation and I could really use some help." White teeth worried her bottom lip, and he shoved his hands farther into his jean pockets rather than reach out and soothe the plump flesh.

What the hell am I thinking?

"Look, lady, I'm sorry, but the answer's no." A flash of hurt and something else—panic?—flitted across her eyes, and he steeled himself from answering the silent call. Sure, he was being an asshole, but he wasn't fit for any type of company.

"I wouldn't normally ask a complete stranger, but I'm at my wit's end. Plus, Willow likes you and I trust her judgment of people better than I trust my own."

A light nudge on his leg had his gaze dropping and meeting a pair of expressive, brown eyes.

Damn dog looked like she could see straight into his soul

and the hurts swirling there. A tiny crack appeared in the reinforced steel wall he'd constructed around his heart.

Remaining firm and saying no to whatever this gal wanted was the only way to guarantee his sanity and maintain his distance from people—and animals.

"What do you need?"

Fuck, seriously? That wasn't what I wanted to say.

"Really?" Her face lit up, the gold flecks in her eyes shimmering with happiness. "You'll really help me?"

Caleb crossed his arms over his chest in an attempt to maintain some distance between them. "Depends on what you need."

"I need you to sit with my dad for a little bit while I go to work."

She wants me to be a babysitter? That can't be right.

"I don't think I heard you correctly."

"Come with me," she said and reached out like she was about to take hold of his hand, pulling back at the last minute. A small part of him couldn't help but feel disappointed she hadn't touched him. Even though their first encounter had been brief, her soft breasts had brushed up against his forearm and a sizzle of lightning had traversed his bloodstream, a sensation he hadn't experienced in a long time. And one he didn't want.

He stood his ground, not moving an inch even though she'd taken a couple of steps down his walkway, as if she expected him to follow her. "Look, Ms. Neighbor *whose name I don't even know.* Did you seriously just ask me to babysit your father?"

She stopped abruptly and blew out a breath; a tendril of dark blonde hair that had escaped her schoolmarm bun flicked in the air before floating down to curl against her cheek. "Hi, I'm Kerry Williams. I know I'm doing this all wrong, and if I weren't so frantic and in a hurry, I wouldn't ask. I don't want to lose my job and if I"—she lifted her hand to look at the simple gold watch adorning her wrist— "don't get to work in the next twenty minutes I'm going to be fired."

The chivalrous nature his parents pounded into him as a kid and the air force had honed over almost twenty years rose up in him and he couldn't ignore it. Against his better judgment, he was going to help his next-door neighbor. He couldn't live with the guilt of knowing his actions had caused her to lose her job. The last thing he wanted was to be responsible for another person's misfortunes. He lived with enough of them already.

Moments passed between them and the smile died on her lips. "Never mind," she murmured and made to move away.

Instinctively, Caleb reached out and placed a hand on her arm, her skin warm and soft under his fingertips. A sensation he did his damnedest to ignore. A light touch, but enough that she paused and turned. He let his hand drop to his side, fighting the need to shake it to dispel the tingles flaring through him.

Her eyebrow rose. "Was there something else you wanted to say?"

"I'll do it even though you've just invited a complete stranger to look after your father. I know *you're* Kerry, but you don't know me," he snapped, the moment still so surreal. "How do you know I'm not some sort of serial killer or something?"

Her eyes widened a fraction, the only indication she hadn't really thought the idea through fully. But in a flash, a small smile spread across her face. Her eyes sparkled in the early evening light, and her plump lips tempted him to taste them. "I trust you because Willow trusts you."

What the hell? Her dog was her barometer? Yep, she was insane.

He shouldn't have gone against his instincts, should have knocked down her request quicker than when Trigger alerted their team to immediate danger in the field. Caleb closed off thoughts of his working dog partner.

Fuck. He needed to remove himself from this whole situation.

Another nudge—the little corgi was rubbing her head back and forth across his leg, as if soothing away his hurts.

God, he should walk away, his sanity wouldn't survive this, but he'd given his word and he never went back on it once he'd given it. He held out his hand, knowing the second she took it in her own, he'd regret it.

"Caleb Bradshaw."

Kerry's smile grew wider.

Shit, attractive women have always been my downfall. Why did I agree to this?

When her hand slid into his, his flesh indeed buzzed at the contact; he was surprised there weren't tiny flashes of lightning sparking between them. "Pleased to meet you, Caleb, and again, thank you so much for helping out. Do you, um, think we can go now? Time is running out for me, and I want to make sure Dad is settled." She pulled her hand out and he closed his fingers in a tight fist. Her entire body language hadn't changed at their touch, so clearly whatever he was feeling was one-sided.

"Yep, let's go."

Kerry cocked her head and then looked at his feet. "Don't you want to, you know, lock your house and grab your phone or whatever?"

"You didn't seem too concerned about that when you all but suggested we leave the second I agreed to helping you."

A faint pink hue bloomed over her cheeks. "We're really making a mess of this, aren't we?" she said ruefully.

Against his better judgment, the corners of his lips quirked up in half a smile. "Seems that way."

"Okay, so how about I go home, try and call one of Dad's friends to see if they can come over in an hour so your whole evening isn't ruined. I can also let Dad know what's going on. While I'm doing that, you can get yourself organized here and then come on over to my place. I can quickly run through everything that he needs. Then I'll go to work."

"Sure." He could do with a few minutes to get his shit together. Not to mention knock some sense into his head at the same time.

She once again headed down the path. "Kerry," he called out, halting her progress. Really, again, why was he doing this? He should just let her go.

"Yes?"

"This is a one-off thing. Don't expect me to babysit your dad again."

Chapter Two

"CALEB, COME IN. Thank you again for doing this."

The aroma of his citrusy aftershave tickled her nostrils. He hadn't been wearing cologne when she'd run into him; she would've remembered the scent for sure. Not that she'd had plenty of opportunity to sniff men's necks.

"It's fine." Tension lines appeared around his eyes, and his tone didn't give her the impression that he was fine with it at all, but she had no choice in the matter.

"Dad is this way," she said as she started down the hallway.

A grunt sounded behind, and she rolled her eyes. Typical male response.

She was pleased to see her dad was still seated in his chair and hadn't attempted to stand to greet Caleb.

"Caleb, this is my father, Ron Williams. Dad, Caleb Bradshaw." She stood back as Caleb strode past her.

"Good to meet you, sir." Caleb's response was clipped and respectful. A little of her doubt about how he would treat her dad evaporated.

"None of this *sir* business. Call me Ron. Thanks for

coming over to babysit me." Dad winked at her. She bit back the urge to poke her tongue out at his cheeky comment.

"Okay, Ron it is. I understand I'll only be here for a little while. Correct?" Caleb sent her a pointed look.

Yeah, yeah she got the hint. The last place he wanted to be was in her house. "Yes, for however long it takes for Eric to get here." She directed her gaze to her father. "You called Eric, didn't you?"

"I did. He's with his daughter but should be here soon. She doesn't live too far away."

"Good." Kerry glanced at her watch again and groaned. "I'm going to be late. I can't afford to lose this job."

"Well, then go." Her father waved his hand in a shooing motion. "We've got this all under control, haven't we, Caleb?"

"Yes, sir."

He'd taken a seat on the couch and Willow was on the ground, her nose resting over Caleb's sneakered feet, a look of concern in her brown eyes. Her dog was telling her something about Caleb, but she didn't know what. And she should. As a therapy dog, Willow was in tune with the emotions of people around her, so she must sense turmoil in Caleb. Or had she picked up on something else? Something that could be harmful to her dad.

"If you're sure?" Still she hesitated in leaving, even knowing every second she stayed at home meant the later she would be to the restaurant.

"Go, Kerry." Her father snagged her gaze and used his best don't-mess-with-me-I'm-your-father tone. "We will be fine."

He was right. She walked over to her dad and laid a hand on his arm. "Thanks again, Caleb," she said to the man who'd come to her rescue, not once, but twice in the last hour.

He nodded and switched his focus to looking out the window. Well then, she'd been dismissed and that was that.

She snatched up her bag, headed to the door while checking the contents for her wallet and sunglasses. Her phone trilled with an incoming text, and she automatically dug the device out of her pocket.

Hi, this is Verna from Angel's Home Help. I'm sorry, but I'm unable to take on the job of looking after your father. I hope you find someone else who's suitable.

"You don't say. Would've been nice if you'd texted me over an hour ago," she muttered and tossed the phone in her bag. Getting someone else to look after her dad would be tomorrow's problem.

IT WAS CLOSE to one a.m. by the time Kerry slotted the key into the back door and entered her kitchen. Willow came running the second she placed her handbag on the counter.

Kerry squatted down and picked her up, snuggling into the coarse dog fur.

"Hey, puppy, why aren't you cuddled up on your grand-daddy's bed, keeping him company?"

Willow licked Kerry's cheek and the fatigue that ate at her bones melted away. "You always make me feel better," she said as she placed the dog on the ground and went to the refrigerator to grab a bottle of water. Her hand stilled when the sound of laughter filtered into the kitchen. "What the hell? Dad's still up?"

Taking a long swallow from her water, she strode down the hallway toward the living room, stopping abruptly. She didn't know which surprised her the most; the fact that Dad appeared happier than he had in a long time or that Caleb was still sitting in the same place he'd been when she'd left for work hours ago.

"I guess my invite to the party got lost?"

"Kerry, sweetie, I didn't hear you come in." Her father's smile was big. "You're not going to believe this, but Eric's future son-in-law, Ethan, lived next door with Caleb. They both serve in the air force."

"Served," Caleb interjected.

Her father waved away Caleb's gruff response. "Semantics. You're just on medical leave."

The humor shining in Caleb's eyes dulled and his lips tensed into a firm line. Definitely something going on there, but it wasn't her place to ask. "Well, that's great. I don't know if Dad told you, Eric, but I've only just moved in and haven't really had a chance to get to know my neighbors. The only reason Caleb is here is because Willow escaped out of the backyard and Caleb found her for me. Then he generously offered to sit with Dad until you came." And, geez, she needed to shut up. She was babbling, and it wasn't anything Eric needed to know.

"I have to admit I was pretty surprised when I saw Caleb here. It's been a great evening though," Eric said as he stood. "But I should be getting home. As I said earlier, Caleb, Ethan's back. I'm sure he'd like to see you. The baby will be here soon too, and then Isabella and Ethan will be getting married. It's going to be a crazy time."

Kerry couldn't drag her gaze away from Caleb. With every word Eric said, Caleb's features tightened and it was like looking at a brick wall. His eyes were as dark as the night sky and the whites of his knuckles stood out on his hands clenched by his sides.

Did he really not like his former roommate? Or was it Ethan's fiancée he had an issue with?

Not your business.

The little voice in her head was correct, but her compassionate side wanted to comfort him. Stupid, considering they'd just met, but Caleb looked lonely even in a room with three other people.

Willow's training kicked in and she waddled over to Caleb and touched his leg with her black nose. If possible, he tensed even more and then stood abruptly, winced, and rubbed a hand down his left thigh.

Interesting.

Her dad had mentioned he was on medical leave and she'd noticed a limp earlier. Was that what he meant by served? So many questions she longed to ask, but she didn't know him well enough to ask him. Instinct told her Caleb was going to do everything possible to avoid stepping foot inside her house again.

"I've got to go. Bye, Eric, it was good to see you again, and to meet you, Ron."

He brushed past her and, before she could think it through clearly, she reached out and halted his progress. Caleb looked at the hand on his arm and then up at her. The pain of whatever he was going through blazed in his eyes. She opened her mouth, closed it, and then opened it again. "Thanks for staying. I really appreciate it."

He nodded brusquely and continued out of the room. Kerry hurried after him to open the front door. The second she did, he was through the gap and striding into the dark night as if a million demons were chasing after him.

Willow barked beside her and Caleb's step faltered a fraction of a second before he disappeared into his own front yard.

A brush against her leg made her look down. "Yeah, puppy, he's hurting for some reason, but I don't think he's ever going to let anyone help him." Not that she had time to help even if the circumstances were different.

Chapter Three

CALEB'S EYES SNAPPED open, his heart raced, and sweat covered his body. As on previous occasions when he'd woken up like this, the memories of the dream he'd been having hovered on the periphery of his psyche like the haze simmering over a hot desert. If he allowed himself to delve into his mind, the images from his dream would be there—but he didn't.

Why did he need to remember the worst day of his life?

The day that changed the path he'd been traveling down. Now here he was, waiting to find out what the next chapter of his life would be while living with the guilt that he hadn't been able to protect Trigger, his K-9 dog.

He'd worked many positions in the security forces division of the air force, but when he moved into the K-9 unit, he'd finally found his home. After almost twenty years in the service, he should've worked his way up the ladder a lot further than he had. The opportunities had been there and he'd been tempted, but in the end, he stayed with Trigger, and their partnership was the longest relationship he'd ever had in his life.

He shifted in bed, to ease a dull ache at the top of his thigh. Flinging back the covers, Caleb swung he legs over the side, grimacing as the movement intensified the pain.

The house was quiet. Too quiet for his liking. After nearly six months of living by himself, he should be used to it. But he wasn't. Being in the military, he'd always been surrounded by people.

What he should do was move. It had been a rash decision to stay in the house once Ethan had informed him his pregnant fiancée and her father would be collecting his things so when he returned from his deployment, he'd move straight in with her. Of course, at the time of the call she hadn't been his fiancée and his former roommate hadn't known he was going to be a father.

Caleb scrubbed a hand down his face. Thinking of Ethan reminded him of the previous evening at his attractive neighbor's house. The way she'd looked when she returned from her job. More strands from her schoolmarm bun had escaped and floated around her face. She looked tired but invigorated, too, as if the job gave her energy to face anything. He'd felt like that once.

Dammit, stop thinking about the past.

He got up and limped to the kitchen. Mornings were always the worst with his leg. Once he'd been moving for half an hour, the tense muscles eased up and he almost forgot about it. He pulled a carton of juice from the fridge and was reaching up to grab a glass from the overhead cupboard when he paused, sure he'd heard something or someone shuffling around on his back porch.

Quieting the jumble of sounds in his mind, he concentrated like he would do on patrol. Yep, there it was again, a definite snuffling sound. The glowing numbers on the microwave informed him it was just before six. The normal time he'd be getting up if he was about to head to base.

But he wasn't and he needed to investigate the sound. It was probably just a feral cat or possum. Worst-case scenario, it was a skunk and he'd have to make sure he didn't do anything to make the critter spray him. Not the best way to start the day.

Heading into the laundry room, he snagged a pair of sweatpants from the pile of folding he needed to do and slipped into them. He found his slide sandals by the back door and grabbed the flashlight he kept on the windowsill in case of emergencies.

Cautiously he opened the laundry room door, which led to the backyard. The beam from the flashlight landed on a pair of eyes, making them glow eerily in the early morning light. But he recognized the eyes. He turned the flashlight off and found the outside light switch, flicking it on.

"Fuck, Willow, what the hell are you doing here again?" The dog padded over to him and sat on her haunches, her brown-and-white coat glistening under the glow of the light bulb, her mouth open as she panted happily at him.

"Willow? Where are you?" He could tell Kerry was trying

not to yell too loudly so as not to wake the whole neighborhood.

Why was her damn dog now finding its way into his backyard?

According to Ron, Kerry and Willow had been living in the house next door to him for two months. He'd heard the dog barking on occasion, but because he'd been keeping to himself, he hadn't seen Kerry or her dog. Now, within the space of twenty-four hours, her dog had found its way into his yard twice.

Yeah, maybe it was time to move. Perhaps a nice apartment complex that didn't allow pets. Now that seemed like a perfect idea.

"Woof."

"Yeah, yeah, that's your owner," he muttered to the dog as he headed across his yard to the fence.

"Willow's over here," he called out.

"Caleb? Is that you?"

"Well it's not friggin' Santa Claus. Yes, it's me." Dammit, he didn't mean to sound so surly. Then again, it was six in the morning. He had reason to be grumpy.

From where he stood he couldn't see Kerry approach, but he heard the faint slap of her feet on the grass. If he got right up to the fence he could probably see over, but he had no plans to do that right now. "Sorry," she said, her voice louder than before. "That was a stupid thing to say. Of course it's you, Caleb. Who else would it be? Our backyards run alongside each other."

Abruptly the flow of words ceased, and his lips twitched into a small smile. He found the way she babbled a little the previous evening kind of endearing. Such a contrast from the way she'd succinctly spoken to him when they first met.

"It's always best to be cautious when you can't see who's speaking to you," he said after the silence between them had stretched beyond the normal pause in conversation.

"I think you're being too nice."

"Woof."

Willow had joined them.

"Willow, girl, what are you doing there?"

"Woof."

"Well, I don't think Caleb appreciates you barging in on him. We're going to have to have a serious talk when I get you."

His smiled grew wider at the one-sided conversation Kerry was having with her dog. He couldn't remember the last time he'd smiled like this. "Why don't I bring Willow over to you and then you can continue this conversation?"

"Oh, that would be great. I'll be out the front of my place in a minute."

Through the pine fence, he could hear her feet slapping as she rushed away. Caleb shook his head and leaned down to scoop up Willow.

"Come on, you. Let's get you to your mom." Before he started thinking that having a dog in his life again was a good thing.

KERRY YANKED HER front door open and rushed down the pathway. She had no idea what had gotten into Willow. There must be a broken fence slat she could wiggle her chubby little body through. A gap that hadn't been there before, because Willow hadn't dug a hole. She'd never been a digger—then again, they hadn't had a backyard at all, so who really knew if her dog was a digger or not?

Willow's collar jingled and Kerry's throat dried as she spied a bare-chested Caleb. She figured he'd have a kick-ass body, being in the air force and all, but hell, the guy looked like his stomach had been sculpted by Michelangelo. In the early morning light, the ridges of his six-pack were highlighted in a tempting package. There were a couple of scars on his chest, and a long, angry-looking one over his shoulder, but they only enhanced his sexiness.

Kerry shook her head. She shouldn't be thinking this way. After being dumped by Winthorn and having to reconstruct the life she'd allowed him to destroy, no way was she losing focus over a hot body. It was going to be a long time before she trusted a man enough to let into her life.

"Willow, what am I going to do with you?" Yeah, that admonishment didn't even slow her dog's roll as she trotted happily beside Caleb. "I'm so sorry she's bothering you,

Caleb. I don't know how she's getting over to your place. She's usually such a good dog and doesn't wander much."

"Guess it's lucky she's coming to my place and not running out onto the road."

Kerry squatted down to check Willow for any signs of scratches or sand in her fur to indicate she'd been digging. It was either that or stare at the bronze expanse of Caleb's chest. And as she'd just lectured herself that men were off-limits looking at her dog was definitely the better option.

"I'll look around the backyard today before I leave for work to see if I can find the hole or gap in the fence she's been sneaking through." But she couldn't keep talking to the ground. She picked up Willow, using her as a pet shield, and focused on the roof of the house across the road. Well, that and Caleb's unscarred shoulder. "Thanks again for bringing her over. It seems you're doing a lot of rescuing for me."

The muscle in his shoulder jumped, the only sign her words affected him somehow. "It's nothing. Just make sure you do find where's she's escaping through. If she keeps coming over I'm going to start..." He clamped his mouth shut and shook his head. "Just keep her in your yard, not mine, and everything will be fine."

He swiveled and marched down her driveway, his limp a little more prominent than the previous evening.

Dang it all, what had she said that upset him?

Willow fidgeted in her arms. "Dammit, Willow, stop it." She tightened her hold and walked back into her house, putting her dog down the second she closed the front door.

"What happened, sweetie?" her dad called out from his room.

Kerry took the time to poke her head in his room. "Willow escaped next door again. I guess there's a hole in the fence or something. I don't know why she's always going over there."

"You didn't go over there uninvited to get her? You know that's dangerous. I know someone who got shot when they went into their neighbor's backyard. Even though they'd known them for years."

Kerry controlled the urge to roll her eyes, but his worrying was sweet. She wouldn't admit that to him just yet. "Of course not. Caleb was outside with her and told me he had her. I told him I'd meet him out the front and then he brought her over."

"Well, that's good. Not that I think Caleb would do anything like shooting you." Dad struggled to sit up and she rushed in to help him. She fluffed his pillows. "God, I hate feeling this helpless," he grumbled.

"Well, next time you decide you're an Olympic downhill skier, you may want to think again."

Willow bounced up and down on her short back legs, trying to jump up to see her dad. Kerry picked her up and placed the animal on the bed. Willow immediately nudged Dad's hand and curled up next to him when he started to pat her.

"She really is a good dog; no wonder you trained her to be a therapy dog."

"Yep, she is, and today is the day we're scheduled go to the veterans' center. We couldn't go last week, so I know a few guys will be happy to see her. But, unless I can get someone from the nursing service to come stay with you, I won't be able to go again."

"What happened with the person who was supposed to turn up last night?"

Kerry sighed and sat down on the bed next to Willow, her hand reaching out to scratch the dog behind her ears. "She sent a text saying she couldn't come. I'll be letting the agency know all about it when I call them in a couple of hours."

"Sweetie, I don't like being an inconvenience. I'm sorry I'm putting you through this."

"Dad, I told you it's not an inconvenience."

"Really?" His eyebrow rose.

She chuckled softly. "Okay, fine, it is a little bit, but I know if I got hurt and needed help you'd be there for me. I'm only returning the favor."

"You know, instead of calling that place again, I've got another idea on who could stay with me."

Kerry's eyes narrowed. That false innocence in her father's tone was too rehearsed. "I don't think I'm going to like this idea."

He had the audacity to grin. "It's the perfect solution.

You go ask Caleb if he'll sit with me."

Clearly her father had lost his mind. The idea was insane. "We can't do that, Dad," she protested. "Last night was a one-off arrangement. It's what we agreed on. I'm not going to impose on him any longer. I may have only just met him, but I think he has some underlying issues that he's probably working on and wants to do so in privacy."

"It won't be for long. You know I've got a doctor's appointment in two weeks, and he's confident the hard cast on my right leg will be removed and I can be put into a boot. He said that break wasn't as severe as the one in my left leg. That means I'll be a bit more mobile and able to do more things for myself."

After the way Caleb had stomped off this morning, the chances of him doing anything for her were as likely as San Antonio getting three days of snow this winter.

"No, Dad," she replied firmly. "I'm not going to ask anything more of Caleb. I already owe him for last night; I don't want to owe him anymore. Now I'm off to fix you breakfast. Once I've done that, I'll call the agency and then see if I can find where this little madam is managing to escape."

Willow looked up at Kerry with an almost smug smile on her face as she walked into the kitchen. If she didn't know better, she'd almost imagine Willow knew exactly what she was doing and had a plan to make Caleb a permanent part of her little doggy world, regardless of his request that she keep Willow as far away from him as possible.

"Don't get any ideas, Willow. I've got my own issues to deal with, and I don't need to be taking on Caleb Bradshaw's."

And she needed to keep reminding herself of that.

Chapter Four

FLICKING A LOCK of hair out of her face, Kerry could find nothing to indicate where Willow had escaped through the fence adjoining Caleb's property. Piles of pulled weeds were dotted down the side of the yard. It wasn't like her garden had been a jungle, but a certain sense of satisfaction filled her at seeing how much neater it looked.

Being neater though didn't explain where Willow was able to get her chubby furry butt through.

Kerry's phone shrilled, momentarily distracting her from her Houdini-esque dog. The number flashing on the screen looked familiar, so she accepted the call.

"Hello?"

"Hi, Ms. Williams. This is DeeDee from Angel's Home Help. How are you?"

Finally, they were calling her back. She'd left a message on their service two hours ago. If this place weren't covered by her dad's insurance she'd tell them where they could go, but since it was and she needed the help, she swallowed her annoyance. "DeeDee, thanks for calling me back."

"Oh, you called us, dear? I wasn't aware. I'm following

up to see how Verna worked out yesterday." The sound of paper shuffling drifted down the phone line. "From what's listed on the order, you're needing help every day for your father while he recovers from an accident. Is that still the case?"

Kerry pinched the bridge of her nose and counted to ten. Seriously, what sort of organization was this if they didn't even know Verna hadn't shown up? "Well, yes, that's still the case, but Verna didn't show up last night. In fact, I was late to work because of her no-show. She sent me a message forty minutes after the time she was due to arrive, saying she couldn't take the job. There was no other explanation."

"Really? That's so unlike Verna. I'm sure there was a valid reason and she'll turn up today. What time is she needed again?"

Normally, Kerry was an even-keeled person. She'd learned that getting angry didn't solve anything. Getting angry at the world because of her mother's illness didn't make it go away, for instance. Maybe if she'd gotten angry on occasion in her relationship with Winthorn, she would've seen the road it was headed down.

But the way DeeDee brushed off her concerns, not to mention assuring her Verna would be there and then asking what time she was needed, made Kerry's blood boil.

If they were this disorganized and blasé about schedules, how the hell could they be trusted to look after her father? No way was she going to put her dad through this. And she wouldn't be able to concentrate at work if she was constantly worried about how Dad was being treated and if his caregiver had run out for an errand and forgotten to come back.

Nope, there was nothing else she could do but to try to get another agency to help her out. Surely, there was more than one organization in her father's network that provided home nursing services.

"You know what, DeeDee? No, we don't need Verna or anyone else from your organization. I won't be recommending you to anyone. Goodbye."

She disconnected the call and clenched her fingers around her phone. Hurling it to the ground might make her feel better, but she couldn't afford to replace a broken phone.

"Having a bad day?"

Kerry's head shot up and she spied Caleb looking over the fence at her, a welcoming smile on his face. Of course, he'd be able to look over it without needing a stepstool. And why did he look so damn happy when he all but threatened her this morning?

"What do you want?"

His smile disappeared. She blew out a breath and consciously loosened her tight muscles. "Sorry, I just had an aggravating phone call."

"I heard."

"I wasn't that loud, was I?" she asked, mortified that she'd been yelling for all the neighbors to hear.

"No, but, like you, I was checking my yard for where

Willow was getting through and I heard you."

"Oh, well, yeah, sorry again for snapping." She was struck again by the handsomeness of his features. The dark brown eyes. His straight nose and his lips, full but not overly so. "Did you find where Willow could be getting through?"

"No. There doesn't seem to be any indication of a hole. As you can see there's no broken fence post either. I'm at a loss."

Kerry approached him, which was a total mistake because now she had to crane her neck to see him. But no way could she retreat, because then she'd look silly.

"I don't understand any of this. I know she can't climb over the fence. She can't even jump on the couch. There has to be some place she's getting through. Some place we haven't found." She tapped her fingers on the fence. "Damn, I was hoping for an easy fix, but it looks like all my problems are going to be more complicated than I want them to be."

"You don't strike me as a person who is anything but in control, and you've probably got a plan in place. However, is there anything I can do to help?"

His offer surprised the heck out of her, and was the last thing she expected from him. She crossed her arms over her chest and raised her eyebrows. "Really? I didn't think you'd want to help after your comments this morning." Even she heard the cynicism in her voice.

His head cocked to the side. "Yeah, well, I'd just woken up and I'm grumpy in the morning until I get my first cup of joe."

It was on the tip of her tongue to challenge the little lie that he was only grumpy in the mornings and lacking caffeine. Even though they'd only met yesterday, she had an inkling his go-to nature was grumpy. "Right, well, thanks for the offer, but I can't impose on you. You've already helped me out of one jam. I'm sure I can get this sorted out with a couple more phone calls." She lifted her phone and looked at the time. "I've got to run. I'll try to see if I can get to the bottom of where Willow is getting through later. Have a good day, Caleb."

She turned and headed toward her back door.

"Wait."

Kerry paused, glanced over her shoulder. "What?"

"I was serious when I said if you need help, just let me know."

The way his fingers curled around the top of the fence, however, told her he hoped like hell she wouldn't take him up on his offer.

That was one thing she'd learned over the last year—while someone might offer to help, there was always a catch and they'd want a payback. She had no plans to be indebted to Caleb.

A SHARP JAB of pain pierced his index finger, and he unfurled the grip he had on the fence. He maintained his gaze on Kerry's retreating figure, and only once she was safely inside her house did he look down at his finger. Imbedded in the soft flesh was a jagged piece of wood.

Great, offer to do something nice for someone and the universe rewarded him with a splinter. Well, to be honest, he'd said the words but was hoping she wouldn't take him up on the offer. So yeah, he deserved being jabbed by a sliver from the fence.

What had he been thinking? He hadn't been thinking. He'd wanted to fix things. Rescue her again, an emotion and compulsion he hadn't experienced in a very long time. Not since before the accident that had changed the course of his life. The accident that took his dog Trigger from him.

A wave of grief swept over him. They'd been a team for so long, not to have him constantly at his side... well, he still wasn't used to it.

He glanced over at Kerry's yard again and spied a doggy face gazing at him from the back porch.

Damn Willow, always showing up when he didn't need her to. He turned his back on the furry creature and headed to his house. What he needed was a shower and... what? After his shower what was he going to do?

A year ago he would've been on base, laughing with the guys. But a job on the Texas/Mexico border had changed everything. He reached down and rubbed the scar on his right thigh while his other hand reached across and fingered the puckered one on his shoulder. He was lucky. Two other guys hadn't been.

"Fuck," he muttered and slammed his back door. Going over the past was never a good thing, and until Willow had turned up on his doorstep, he'd been dealing well, not having anything to do with dogs.

As a roommate, Ethan had known what Caleb had gone through, so he never talked about his K-9 partner. When Caleb visited the base, he had been in a different area to the dog training facility, where Ethan and the other guys from his platoon would be.

The house phone rang loudly in the silence. A foreign sound, considering the last time anyone had phoned him on the landline had been about two months ago, and that was just a marketing call. Which this probably was, so he let the machine pick it up.

"Uh, hi, Caleb, this is Ron. Ron Williams. I was with you and Eric Knowles last night. Um, I got your number from Eric, so I hope you don't mind me calling. Geez, if Kerry knew what I was doing, she'd snatch the phone away."

Caleb smiled. He could definitely imagine Kerry doing that to her father. But he was intrigued as to why Ron was calling him. In two strides, he reached the counter and snatched up the phone.

"I'm here, Ron, what can I do for you?"

"Caleb. Great. You know…"

"Dad, who are you talking to?" Uh-oh, Kerry had sprung

her father. Now this was going to get interesting.

"Umm, no one."

"Right. I can tell by the look on your face that you're up to no good. How about you be straight with me?"

The melancholy that had been pervading Caleb's bones disappeared as he eavesdropped on the exchange between father and daughter. He would like to see the look on Kerry's face. He could imagine her arms would be crossed over her small but tantalizing chest.

Her short pajamas this morning and workout clothes he'd seen her wear in the yard had defined her body in a way that the smart pants and button-down work shirt last night had hidden.

He needed to shut down that thought.

"Dad, I'm waiting."

Over the phone line, Ron's breath puffed out. "Fine, I'm talking to Caleb."

"Caleb? Not our neighbor Caleb. Please tell me you're not."

Her horror would've been an insult if he hadn't seen or heard her skepticism to his offer to help her. He supposed he deserved it; he hadn't been friendly when he handed Willow back earlier either.

"Give me that phone now, Dad." The sound of the phone exchanging owners scratched in his ear.

"Caleb? Is that you?"

"Hey, Kerry, it's me." He bit back a smile. Dammit, his

cheek muscles hadn't had a workout like this in a while.

"Oh, my God, I don't know what Dad is thinking calling you. First Willow and now my dad is bothering you. I'm so sorry. I'll make sure he doesn't do it again." Her words rushed out faster than a bullet train. She had no reason to be embarrassed, but given his abrupt comments to her this morning and a few moments ago, along with her conviction that she wasn't going to disturb him again, he could understand it.

"Kerry, stop, it's fine. Has Willow gone missing again?"

The dog had been outside before he'd disappeared inside, so given how wily the little creature was, if she'd escaped again, he wouldn't be surprised.

"No, she's still here. In fact, we should be going to veterans' center so she can work, but we won't now."

Kerry was going to the veterans' center? He'd been asked to visit that place during his medical leave. So far, he'd avoided it like the plague. He had his own shit to sort out; he would be of no use to anyone down there. The universe was clearly trying to tell him something, though. Why else in the space of twenty-four hours would he see Ethan's future father-in-law, a military vet himself, and have a dog turn up twice on his property when he'd been avoiding dogs as best he could?

"Why aren't you going?" he asked. Did he really want to know?

"It's nothing that concerns you. I'll get it sorted out."

Her voice was harried. Now he knew why her father was calling. "You can't get anyone to look after Ron, can you?"

He heard her sharp intake of breath. He'd hit the nail on the head. "Why do you say that?"

"You forget, I overheard your side of your phone conversation while you were in the yard."

"Fine, you're right. The other agency in Dad's insurance network doesn't have anyone available to care for him. But it's not an issue—I'll sort it out. And it really isn't your problem, Caleb. Again, I'm sorry Dad disturbed you."

"Ask him." Caleb made out the words spoken from the background.

"No, Dad, I'm not going to. We will work it out." Kerry didn't try hard to muffle her voice. Her determination not to bother him was admirable, but it was too late. He was aware of the situation, and even though he'd like nothing better than to disconnect the call and get on with his life, he couldn't walk away. For almost twenty years, he'd put service above himself. It was time he remembered that.

"How long will you be gone?" he asked.

"What?"

"How long will you be at the center?"

"Why do you want to know?"

He sighed and took a deep breath. "Because I'm here, and you need help."

"Wait a second. Are you offering to come and sit with Dad?"

"Yes." Even saying the word surprised the hell out of him. He'd done his level best to avoid people over the last couple of months, an easy feat with dumping Amy and Ethan on deployment and no longer living in the house. "Don't worry about getting someone from an agency to look after your dad. I'll do it until he's in a position to look after himself." And that was an even bigger accomplishment.

"Bu-but, I-I. Why?"

Yeah, that was a good question, and he didn't quite know the answer to it either. "It seems to me that whatever you're doing with Willow is important, not to mention your job, too. If I can help you worry about one less thing, then let me do it."

"I don't know what to say. I can't impose. It wouldn't be fair."

"Just say yes, Kerry. I'm okay doing this for you."

"If you're sure."

"I am."

"Well, then, yes, thank you, Caleb. I appreciate the offer. I know Dad will be happy to spend time with you again. He enjoyed your company last night."

He ignored the last bit. It was easier than admitting to himself he'd felt the same way talking to Ron and Eric. But last night was an anomaly. "I can be there in fifteen minutes. Will that work?"

"That's perfect. Thank you."

Caleb disconnected the call before he said something else

out of character. Who was this person, and would the real Caleb Bradshaw please stand up?

Not true. This is you—you just forgot about it for a little while.

Caleb ignored the voice and the truth ringing in every word. He wasn't that person anymore. He could do this small favor and then, once Ron was up and about, he'd walk away and retreat back to his bubble. The one where nothing hurt.

Chapter Five

A WEEK LATER, Kerry stood to the side of the communal room at the veterans' center and watched Willow do her stuff. At the moment, she was sitting on a couch next to a man while he played chess. The man's hand was clutching the scuff of her neck, his leg moving up and down in vigorous movements. Sensing his agitation, Willow lifted her head and laid it down on the leg, stilling the movements immediately. His hand loosened the grip on her short brown-and-white fur and began to stroke. Even from her vantage point, she could see the tension drain out of him with every stroke down Willow's back.

"Well, hello there, Kerry. I forgot you were going to be here today. How's Ron?"

Kerry straightened and glanced over at the man standing next to her. "Hey, Eric, Dad's good. Thanks for coming over last week. He really enjoyed your company."

Eric waved at a group of men of varying ages clustered around a table, playing poker. "I enjoyed it too. I was surprised to see Caleb there. Ethan couldn't believe it either. He said it has been an effort to get Caleb to leave the house ever since his accident. The only time Caleb left the house was to go to and from rehab or if Ethan's friends had get-togethers."

Spindles of curiosity popped up inside of her, but she pushed them aside. What happened to Caleb was his business, and if he, at some stage in the future, wanted to tell her, then she would listen. In her mind, it would be a betrayal to question Eric about the man who was doing her a favor. "I'm extremely grateful for him helping me when he didn't know me. And he's still helping me."

"What do you mean?" asked Eric.

"Caleb offered to look after Dad until he was more mobile. From what Dad's been saying, they've been having a good time."

Eric's mouth hung open. "Caleb's helping your dad?"

"Yes. Over the last week he's taken him out or stayed at the house with him when I've been working at the restaurant or here with Willow."

"Caleb should come here. It would do him good," Eric murmured.

Whether that was true or not, it wasn't up to her to make Caleb do anything. The man could deal with his problems without her interference. Whenever she and Willow came home, her dog would waddle over to where Caleb was sitting and flop down on the ground, her snout resting on his shoes. And every single time, Caleb tensed and moved his feet away. Or stood abruptly and declared he needed to get home. It was clear he didn't need or want help.

"Why do you think Caleb needs to be here?" she asked Eric, against her better judgment.

"When you're in the service, you see and experience things the everyday citizen doesn't." He paused and canted his head toward Willow. "PTSD is insidious, and the more we talk about it, the more we can help the people suffering. You and Willow being here helps the guys acclimatize back into civilian life."

Kerry's mind churned, trying to pick out the underlying message Eric was attempting to give her. If he was suggesting Caleb had some PTSD issues and she could help, he had another thing coming. Dealing with someone displaying signs of PTSD was above her pay grade. Heck, how many times had she got frustrated with her dad and had to count to fifteen before answering him?

Nope, Caleb was better off seeking help from someone other than her. "You can't make someone do something they don't want to," she said finally.

Eric smiled and patted her on the hand. "You're right, but you can encourage."

"Eric, are you planning on standing there all day flirting, or are you gonna come play cards?" an older gentleman yelled at them and Kerry rolled her eyes at his comment.

"Shut up, Derek, I'll be right over." Eric looked back at her. "Think about what I said. I think you have more influence than you give yourself credit for."

He joined the men, slapping a couple on the back before taking a seat. Kerry had yet to meet his daughter and Ethan. Eric and her dad had met on a hunting trip, before her dad decided to try skiing. He was definitely making the most of his retirement. Although he probably hadn't planned on breaking his legs and curtailing his sense of adventure for a while.

She glanced at her watch; it was time to collect Willow. This was always the tough part of her visit. Willow never seemed to want to leave her friends, and they didn't want her to go either. But as in all therapy situations, Willow's presence was part of their journey to recovery. Nine times out of ten, most of the guys ended up getting their own dogs after a few months, usually rescue dogs from the local shelter. It warmed her heart knowing that two lost souls had found a home with each other.

Eric's words about encouraging Caleb floated through her mind. Perhaps she would invite Caleb to come on a visit with her when Dad could be left alone again—maybe.

THE SECOND KERRY opened the door, Willow scampered through the gap, her furry butt wiggling from side to side as she raced toward the front room. Kerry smiled. Corgis had attitude, and Willow had it in spades.

Setting her keys on the hook by the door, she wandered

into the kitchen and headed for the fridge. The previous evening, the desserts chef at the restaurant had given her a piece of chocolate cake. She'd hidden it in the back so her dad wouldn't find it. Not that he could have inspected the contents of the fridge—he was still laid up.

She'd been craving the delicious-looking cake the whole trip home. Leaning in, she moved a couple of take-out containers and a package of lettuce before she spied the white box.

"Ah-ha, there you are. Come to me, my pretty."

She slammed the fridge shut and looked up, almost dropping the cake at the sight of Caleb leaning nonchalantly against the doorframe. His arms crossed over his impressive chest. The sky-blue T-shirt he wore contrasted nicely against his shaggy brown hair. His lips were quirked in a half smile.

"Umm, hi, Caleb. I didn't hear you come in."

He pulled himself away from the door and took two steps into the kitchen. "I'm not surprised. Your concentration was elsewhere." He nodded toward the white pastry box in her hand. "What ya got there?"

She held it up. "This? It's nothing."

He closed the distance between them. "Is that right? If it's *nothing* then you won't mind showing me, will you?"

"You won't like it," she said holding the box close. When it came to cake, especially chocolate cake, she was very possessive.

"How do you know?" he challenged.

Invisible sparks of attraction flared like solar bursts. Her heart picked up speed to beat uncontrollably against her chest. "You don't seem the type to like sweet things."

"You'd be surprised. What is it? Cheesecake? Brownie?"

"Nope. And nope."

He leaned a little closer his citrus scent assailed her nostrils and her eyes drifted shut.

Mmmm, orange chocolate cake. Now that would be delicious.

She sucked in a breath and opened her eyes, keeping them focused firmly on the middle of his chest. Which was a bad idea, because images of him without his shirt had been a constant in her dreams.

Okay, stop. Remember, you're not doing this.

Yeah, her subconscious had a mind of its own. What she needed to remember was in another week or so, Caleb would go back to his own life and she'd continue on with hers. Nothing more and nothing less.

Right now, her life was all about her. No one else. She was doing her own thing. She didn't need a man to prop her up anymore.

"Is it chocolate cake? Yeah, I bet it is." The words floated against her cheek and in that second he sounded like Joey from *Friends* saying *how* you *doing*?

Was Caleb flirting with her?

Now she was imagining things, wasn't she?

Kerry looked up from her study of his chest and their

gazes connected. His brown eyes were warmer than a hot chocolate on a cold winter's day. In slow motion, his hand landed on her shoulder, the touch generated a smoldering fire inside of her, just waiting for the fuel to make it a roaring blaze.

"Is it, Kerry?"

She swallowed hard. "Is it what?"

He tapped the white box with his free hand. "Chocolate cake."

Her tongue darted out and moisten her dry lips. His own tongue repeated her action. "Yes." The word whispered out of her.

An invisible lasso had banded around them and, as if the invisible cowboy that looped it pulled to tighten the rope, she swayed toward him and went up on tiptoe as Caleb lowered his head.

Oh my God, he's going to kiss me.

The thought ricocheted around her mind like a Mexican jumping bean. As their lips were about to meld, a crash echoed around the house, followed by cursing and Willow barking.

Kerry sprang away, her breath sawing in and out as though she'd run a marathon. They hadn't even kissed. What would happen if they actually did?

"I, uh, I'd better go see what's happened."

"Yeah, you should. And I should probably go home."

Neither of them moved.

"Kerry, I need some help," her father yelled just as Willow scampered into the room. It was the kick she needed to break her gaze from Caleb.

She cleared her throat and placed the cake box on the counter. "Umm, thanks for being with Dad today."

Caleb shrugged. "You don't have to keep thanking me. I volunteered, remember?"

She sighed. Things had just gotten awkward between them because of their almost kiss. No way now was she going to ask him to join her at the veterans' center no matter how much Eric might have thought it was a good idea.

CALEB OPENED THE refrigerator and looked at the bare shelves. He needed to get his shit together and go to the store. Then again, if he didn't have to help with Ron every day, he could've replenished his stocks.

And pigs could fly.

Ethan was the one who had usually kept things stocked, so for the last six months Caleb had been existing on takeout and the very rare trip to the store.

He scrubbed a hand down his face.

When had he become so pathetic?

When had he given up on living?

The answer was simple. The day over a year ago when his life had blown up on the Mexico/Texas border. Where a bunch of drug runners and people smugglers had taken on him and the small group of men he'd been with. They'd won, but one of the casualties had been too much for him to deal with. His dog, Trigger, shot in the crossfire while protecting him. He now had bullet fragments lodged in his thigh muscle, and his right shoulder would never be the same.

"Fuck!" he yelled into the empty house, the sound echoing around him.

Snatching up his keys and grabbing a jacket from the hook by the back door, he headed out to his car. He didn't normally hang out at bars, but tonight he had a need for something other than his own company. He liked having the odd beer, but never drank excessively. Alcohol had never solved any problems, and many times during the dark days of his recovery, he'd been tempted to sink into the pit of an alcoholic blur, like so many others when life handed them lemons. Only he wouldn't have been able to stop if he started, and while his life was as shattered as his shoulder bone, he wasn't going to give up on it.

He fired up the engine and reversed into the street, ignoring the welcoming light shining in his neighbor's front room.

Every day, he wished Willow hadn't wandered into his backyard and he hadn't met Kerry. His life would certainly be less complicated if his neighbor had remained a stranger.

Her sweet orange blossom scent in the kitchen had called

to him like a siren's song. Teasing her had seemed so natural. An invisible thread seemed to draw them together, and her luscious pink lips begged for him to taste them. To find out if they were firm or soft. He predicted they'd be a combination of both.

His dick twitched against the zipper of his jeans. Walking into a bar with a hard-on wasn't a good look. Maybe when he got out of the car a gust of cold breeze would temper his ardor—which was as unlikely as Texas having a mild summer.

Thinking about Kerry had to stop for his sanity. Caleb had made a solemn vow to keep his emotions under control and not give anyone else the power to hurt him the way Trigger's loss had cut into him.

And then, just when he thought life couldn't hit him harder while he was down, his father had died in a fiery wreck on his way to San Antonio during Caleb's recovery. Losing the person he'd looked up to his whole life on top of losing Trigger almost sent him to the dark depths of hell. Guilt for his part in these two deaths still ate away at him.

Caleb blew out a deep breath and pushed the thoughts away. For the next two hours, he was going to nurse one beer and have a greasy burger and fries. The taste of the food didn't matter. He just hoped the place had loud music so it would drown out the incessant thoughts of his past hurts and, now, his sexy neighbor.

His wishes were answered the second he opened the

door. From the outside, the place looked like a rundown building that should be condemned by the health department. On the inside, loud music resounded. Peanut shells coated the floor and the smell of stale beer and grilled food assailed his nostrils. It was the perfect place to blend into the shadows.

"Hey there, just take a seat and I'll be with you shortly," a pert waitress said as she strode past, balancing a tray weighed down with beer bottles.

He followed her direction and spied the long table filled with a group of college students. By the amount of empty beer bottles already scattered across the tabletop, a celebration was in progress. One of the guys tried to grope the waitress, but she deftly moved out of the way, as if she was used to it. And she probably was, but that didn't make it right.

Not thinking through his actions clearly, he walked toward an empty booth adjacent to the rowdy group. The sound of peanut shells disintegrating beneath his boots was satisfying.

As he sat, he counted ten guys squashed around the table.

"What can I get ya?" the waitress asked.

"I'll take a glass of whatever you've got on tap and"—he paused and glanced at the chalkboard menu—"a barbeque bacon cheeseburger, with fries, hold the pickles."

"Coming right up." She sashayed away.

"Twenty bucks says you can get her tonight, Jed," one of the guys from the table remarked loud enough for her to hear.

Her back straightened and Caleb tensed. Anything might happen.

The waitress glanced over her shoulder and a look of disdain crossed her features. "Baby, you've got no chance. And say something like that again and y'all will be out on your asses so quick you won't know what hit you."

The guys looked like they were going to object, but Caleb sent them his *don't fuck with me* look and they settled back down. The look probably wasn't necessary; in his peripheral vision he'd noted the bartender and a couple of guys seated at the bar had been watching the scene unfold too.

"What you staring at, old man?" one of the guys sneered at him.

Caleb knew better than to engage. He'd come here to get away from his thoughts. Getting into a bar fight wasn't on his horizon. "Minding my own business."

"Keep it that way."

His beer was plonked down on the scratched wood in front of him. "Don't mind them. If they get too out of control, Troy and company will handle them."

"Believe me, I have no intention of getting involved."

The rest of the evening passed by without incident. Whether it was because of what the waitress said or because of him watching the rowdy group most of the night, Caleb didn't know. What he did know was that it had felt good to be back in protective mode again. While it might have just been a bar, it reminded him of all the good he'd done in the air force.

Decision time was looming. A final hearing by the medical board on his injury was due soon. He'd completed his required rehab a couple of months ago and now he was waiting to find out if he could stay in the air force in a new position or be medically discharged with full benefits. He was still young at almost thirty-eight. Sitting behind a desk pushing papers had never been his idea of a great job. Being in the air force was all he'd ever known. He hadn't been a brainiac at school. He'd done enough to get by, which was why joining the military would guarantee him a job and a regular paycheck. Serving his country was a bonus he hadn't expected to hit him deep in the heart.

But he had expected to be an airman for life. Now the decision might be taken out of his hands.

As he pulled into his driveway, he glanced at Kerry's house. Darkness shrouded the structure and a sense of disappointment filled him.

What had he been hoping? That she'd be waiting on her front porch for him to return? He shook his head as he got out of the car. Now that was a crazy thought.

He was at a crossroads in his life. The career he loved was in tatters and the idea of being stuck in a role he didn't love appealed about as much as a wet blanket on a cold day. Getting involved with a woman right now wasn't conducive to anything.

He had to find something else he could be passionate about. The problem was, he had no idea what that would be.

Chapter Six

THE HUMIDITY HIT Kerry the second she opened her front door. Wasn't it supposed to be fall? Yeah, fall in Texas was one day in November, maybe a week at the most. Winter was another blink-and-miss-it season as well.

Clipping the leash on Willow's collar, she skipped down the path and headed for the sidewalk. A brisk walk was what she needed to clear her thoughts. Sleep had been as elusive as that Texas winter. Every time she had closed her eyes, she saw Caleb's face. The slight uptick of his mouth in the sexy, teasing way. The way the corners of his eyes had crinkled as he talked to her. She'd even put the cake back in the fridge. The thought of eating it hadn't appealed as much as it had earlier.

She would make sure to keep her interaction with Caleb today to a minimum. Business, strictly business, was how she had to think about their relationship. She couldn't let herself think about it being more. After having her life uprooted in a way she'd never thought possible, getting involved with a complex man like Caleb was the last thing she needed or wanted.

Today she had a full day at work, before the cards tournament at the veterans' center this evening. She'd be taking Willow because memories of playing cards while on deployment could be a powerful reminder of what the men had been through. PTSD came in all different shapes and forms, and the unlikeliest of things could set off an attack.

It broke Kerry's heart when these strong people crumpled in front of her. They'd sacrificed so much for her and her country. Training Willow to be a therapy dog, specifically to work with veterans, was her way of giving back.

It wasn't as if she had any family members who'd served in the various forces. But that didn't mean she didn't appreciate all they'd given up and lost over their time in the military.

Willow pulled on her leash, jarring Kerry from her thoughts.

"Stop." Willow obeyed immediately. Her dog never pulled on the lead. Even as a puppy, the dog had always trotted beside Kerry, never attempting to dart away. "You don't pull, Willow, and you know that."

Her dog let out a little bark and her tail wagged. Kerry looked across the street and saw a tall man walking, a slight limp marring his stride. Her breath caught in her throat.

Caleb.

He was wearing a tank top that clung to his torso. The jogging shorts accentuated the long length of his legs. From where she stood, it appeared that his hair was plastered to his head, as if he'd been running.

Willow barked loudly, and because Kerry's attention was fixed on him, she caught the way his head turned quickly in her direction before looking forward. His stride faltered and he clenched his fist.

She still didn't understand why he was so averse to dogs.

She opened her mouth to call out a greeting, but Caleb lowered his head in avoidance and continued on his way.

Well, that was rude. It wasn't like that they were complete strangers.

"I don't think I'll ever understand him. And why should I?" she asked Willow.

Her dog yipped, but it wasn't a helpful answer to her theoretical question. "Let's go, Will. I've got a busy day, and I don't need to be worried about my surly neighbor. And you need to leave him alone today, do you understand?"

She was standing in the middle of the sidewalk talking to her dog. Who did that? She did, apparently.

The rest of the walk passed without incident, but for half a heartbeat she paused at Caleb's house. Should she ask him why he ignored her on the street or let it pass?

In the end, she walked back to her place. There was no point in arguing with him. She needed his help for a few more days. Then they could get on with their own lives and never have anything to do with each other ever again.

"I'M GLAD YOU decided to come out tonight, Dad. I think it will do you good." Kerry wheeled her father up the ramp to the front door of the veterans' center, Willow sat on her dad's lap looking like the Queen of England. Eric had called earlier, inviting Dad to join game night. Apparently, his daughter Isabella and her fiancé Ethan were thinking of going, but he warned it may not happen if Isabella felt too tired.

Kerry was intrigued at maybe meeting the man who could've been her neighbor. Was he similar to Caleb? The strong, quiet type who kept to himself and buried any hurts deep inside? Would he, if she asked, tell her about Caleb?

Stop it.

The little voice in her head practically yelled the words at her. She'd been warring all day with that voice. Even though she'd tried to convince herself that once her dad was better she'd have nothing to do with Caleb, it was a lie. He was her neighbor; she couldn't avoid him forever, not after he'd gone out of his way to provide her with help when he didn't have to.

"I'm looking forward to it, too. It's going to fun. Although I don't feel like I should be here, seeing as I'm not a veteran and all."

"Had you ever considered going into the military?" she asked as the double glass doors whispered open and she rolled them over the threshold.

"No, I didn't. I knew plenty of guys from my high

school class who enlisted. Not all of them made it through basic training. I knew my limitations. If I'd joined, I'd have been one of the ones quitting after the first day." He reached up and patted her hand curled around the plastic handle. "My skills were better off in building things. Besides, if I'd joined the military, I'd never have met your mom."

Kerry smiled as they continued in. Her parents met when Dad had been fixing the front porch railing on her mom's parents' house. Her mom adamantly denied that she'd deliberately tripped over a nonexistent raised plank so her father would catch her and sweep her up in his arms. Deep down, Kerry knew her mom had done just what her father said she'd done. Theirs had been a great romance, from the day they laid eyes on each other to the day her mother's last breath left her body.

A sigh rippled through her. She wanted that for herself. Mistakenly, she'd thought she'd had it with Winthorn Hartigan the third. He'd swept her off her feet, put her on a pedestal, too. The difference? Dad was quite happy for Mom to do her own thing, and he supported her. Winthorn had started off that way, but little by little, he'd changed the dynamics and Kerry had been so blind she hadn't seen how he'd manipulated her until she was molded into what he wanted and had become a yes person. The type of person she never imagined she could be.

Being dumped and called a usurper and leech had been a shock, and so very devastating.

She'd been at the lowest point she'd ever been in her life when he kicked her out.

Raucous laughter pulled her from the dark hole she had been tumbling into. That part of her life was over. She'd clawed her way back to being the independent woman she was. She had a house. A good job. A wonderful companion in Willow and a parent who loved her unconditionally.

What more could she want?

"Ron, you didn't tell me you were coming tonight."

Her head shot up, almost giving herself whiplash. "Caleb?" She gasped. What was he doing here? Hadn't Eric told her he always turned down the man's invitations?

What the hell was going on?

Willow took the initiative to jump off Dad's lap and waggle over to Caleb, where she butted up against his leg until he leaned down and scratched her head. How dare he ignore her on the street and now act like everything was normal?

"So, she's good enough to acknowledge now, is she?" she snapped at him as she took the two steps needed to get in his personal space. "What's so different about now than this morning when she barked a hello to you?"

When he went to open his mouth, she held up her hand. "I don't want to hear your lame excuses."

Kerry bent and scooped up her dog, holding her close to her chest. Willow licked her face and snuggled her head against her shoulder. Kerry closed her eyes and let out the deep breath.

"Well, this is a bit awkward, isn't it?" Dad commented behind her.

Damn, she'd made a scene and making scenes so wasn't what she did. Not to mention being rude to him. She should apologize for her reaction, even if it had felt good to let off a little steam. Stubbornness kept the apology lodged in her throat. Caleb was a mass of contradictions she didn't understand, but on some level, she wanted to unravel everything that made him the way he was. God, she didn't have time for these thoughts when her focus was on being reliant on no one but herself.

"Bad day," she muttered, which was a little white lie, but she had no desire to explain her outburst to anyone.

"I can relate. I should apologize for this morning. I have no excuse for the way I acted. I'm sorry, Kerry."

The last thing she expected was an apology from him. Again, another example of his contradictory behavior. She couldn't deny it was nice to receive an apology just the same.

"Thank you." She lowered Willow back on her dad's lap. "Shall we go in?"

Caleb nodded and set off down the short hallway toward the game room. Her dad placed his hand over hers.

"I'm not sure what's going on with you two, but Caleb has been really helpful. Remember that."

"I know, Dad. I just, well, he ignored us on the street this morning and that hurt, considering the time you two have spent together."

"There's a lot of pain inside of him. He thinks he hides it from me, but I've seen the way he retreats inside of himself. That's when Willow goes over to him. Every single time. And it's in those moments that he automatically reaches out and rests his hand on her. Pats her, and I see the tension ease in his muscles. I don't think he even realizes he's doing it, because when he comes back to himself, he snatches his hand away and gets up to put distance between them."

"How come you've never told me this?"

"Because I didn't think it was relevant."

"And now you do?"

"Yes."

Her father was being mysterious and she wasn't sure she liked it. "Why?"

"Because it might help you understand him a little better."

"Stop right there, Dad. Don't go getting ideas."

Dad was well aware of what happened between her and Winthorn. At the time, Dad had been all fired up to get up in her former boyfriend's face. Her parents' support, even with Mom in the last stage of her life, had been wonderful. But part of Kerry still wondered if her mom died disappointed that Kerry and Winthorn hadn't walked down the aisle. She thanked her lucky stars that Winthorn had dumped her. Free from him, she was now aware of how she'd let him take over all aspects of her life. Of how she'd fallen into an abusive relationship and hadn't even known it at the time.

She was never going to let that happen again.

Caleb was way too complicated and, even though she didn't know the full story, he had a truckload of baggage she wasn't ready to take on.

"I'm not getting any ideas, sweetie, but you're too young to be always alone."

"I like my own company, Dad and, currently, I'm not alone. I have you and Willow." She leaned down and kissed him on the cheek. They'd come for game night, not for deep and meaningful conversations. Time to get back to the purpose of their evening. "Come on, let's go in. I'm ready to let Willow do her thing and partake in a little bit of gaming myself."

Not waiting for an answer, Kerry headed in the direction Caleb had gone. So what if seeing him tonight had been unexpected? It would be quite easy for her to avoid him if she wanted to.

And tonight, she planned to.

Chapter Seven

KERRY'S LAUGHTER WASN'T loud, considering the voices in the room were a hundred decibels over normal conversation levels, but Caleb heard it all the same. He'd been aware of her the second she'd walked into the room with her dad. Every table she went to, he knew it. He was also very conscious of the fact she was avoiding him. Ron had been playing poker with him most of the evening. The second Caleb sat himself down at the last seat available at their table, Kerry had excused herself. Willow, on the other hand, had made numerous visits back to his side.

The dog was amazing. Ron had told him about her being a therapy dog, and it wasn't the first time Caleb had heard of them, but he'd never seen one in action. So this was why she always approached him when he drifted off to dark places on those evenings with Ron.

Unfortunately, he couldn't pet her this evening. It would be too obvious to the watchful eyes of the people in the room.

"Do you plan on playing this round or are you going to stay where you are with the fairies?"

Caleb raised his eyes to find Eric and Ron as well as the two other occupants of the table watching him, speculation rife in their eyes.

He looked down at the cards in his hand. He supposed he had a reasonable chance of winning this round, but his heart just wasn't in it.

A flash of blue exiting the side door caught his attention, and he tossed his cards on the table. "Nah, I'm out." He pushed his chair back. "I'm going to get some air."

Lame excuse and so transparent he wasn't surprised the men at the table didn't laugh at him. He caught Ron's narrowed gaze and gave the man a slight nod. The message was clear in his eyes. Tread carefully, and if he did anything to hurt his daughter, Caleb would deal with his wrath.

Caleb weaved his way through the tables, willing this compulsion to follow Kerry to go away. He even attempted to swerve in a different direction, but a few moments later he found himself standing by the door she'd exited through.

Fighting the inevitable was ridiculous. He'd known the second he'd seen her standing in the hallway that he would seek her out sometime during the night. He'd battled and won the urge not to cross the street this morning and speak to her—fighting it twice in one day was impossible. Deep down, he knew he should stay away from her and her dog. The last thing she needed was him dulling the aura of beauty that surrounded her with his demons and doubts. Yet, she also represented hope. Hope there was still light and laughter in the world.

A familiar brush against his pants eased the tension. Willow's little doggie face stared up at him with concern. He'd been able to read Trigger like a book. When Trigger's tongue lolled to the side of his open mouth, Caleb had known his partner was happy. Dogs had personalities, and the little one at his feet had been working her magic on many people in the room tonight. Why wouldn't she want to work her magic on him?

Why did he keep fighting it?

He reached down and scratched her behind the ears, an action he'd seen a lot of men in the room do that evening. "I'm okay, Willow. Go help someone who really needs it. I'm going to find Kerry."

Her head cocked to the side the second he mentioned her owner's name. Giving his leg another nudge, as if to say, *Kerry? You're going to see Kerry? Okay then.* With another pat to her head, Caleb straightened and gripped the door handle, waiting until Willow trotted away, her little corgi butt swishing from side to side. Lightness filled him; she really did have a self-confident attitude.

When he spied her settled with another veteran, he opened the door and walked out into the darkness. The song of the night birds sounded foreign to his ears after the loud buzz of conversation. He breathed in a large lungful of air, before blowing it out in a rush.

"Was it getting too much for you? Are you doing okay?"

A familiar voice sounded to the left of him and he turned, seeing Kerry standing in the shadows cast by the building.

Drawn by the invisible thread between them, he made his way to where she stood. "No, I came out to see you," he murmured.

This close, he was able to see the way her eyes widened. Hell, he'd even surprised himself with his words.

"Does Dad need me?" she asked, a hint of worry entering her voice.

"No, Ron's fine. I left mid-hand, but he's been cleaning everyone out. I think Eric regrets inviting him here."

Her husky chuckled rippled over him like the night air. "That's Dad. I probably should've told Eric—before Mom needed constant monitoring as her condition deteriorated, he'd go out with some construction buddies and play poker until all hours of the morning."

"I'm sorry about your mom," he said.

She shrugged, as if brushing off an annoying bug, but he'd seen the grief fill her eyes. "Thanks. I still miss her."

"Let's take a walk." The last thing he wanted was for someone else to come out and spy them together. Not to mention overhear their conversation. He couldn't explain the need to have her all to himself. He'd never experienced this need with any of the women he'd dated.

Her gaze darted to the door as she twisted away from him. If that wasn't an indication she wanted to stay far away from him, he didn't know what was.

"Please, Kerry, take a walk with me. If you're worried about Ron, he's with Eric, and Willow's there too."

In the muted light he saw her brow furrow for a heart-beat before smoothing out.

"Um, sure." She shoved her hands in her jeans pockets.

One hurdle jumped, but, damn, he'd wanted to take her hand. Instead, he settled for placing his palm on her lower back, guiding her away from the building.

They walked for a few minutes before he spied a wooden bench beneath a large oak tree. "Shall we sit over there?" he asked.

"Sure, I don't think there are any squirrels around who'd like to play hit the human on the head with a nut."

He chuckled as he sat down beside her. "Had that happen to you often?"

"No, but it happened to a friend of mine." She leaned back, and he placed his arm across the back of the bench. Her hair brushed against his arm.

"They're aggressive little creatures. I don't know why people think they're cute."

"Well, they can be when they want to be."

Talking about squirrels was the last thing he expected, although he supposed it was better than the weather. What he really needed to do was apologize again for ignoring her this morning. After flirting with her in her kitchen, he could understand why his coldness annoyed the crap out of her.

"I know I said it earlier tonight, but I want to say sorry

again for what I did this morning. There are no excuses for treating you with such disrespect. It's not who I am. Or how my parents raised me. Nor what I learned in the air force."

She adjusted her position so that she was facing him. His hand now cupped her shoulder; the silky fabric of her blouse teased his fingers. "You've been looking after my dad for a while now. I've seen you often enough. So, yeah, I was a little angry with the way you treated me. It made no sense."

Caleb shifted to curl a few silky strands of her hair around his finger, trying to avoid answering her for as long as he could. "I'm at a crossroads with my life. Things have happened that have thrown me into a spin, and I'm still struggling to get out of it."

As far as explanations went, that wasn't very clear, but there were things he didn't want to go into. Events in his past that hurt to even think about, let alone tell a woman he'd only known for a short time. He willed her to understand. To accept his explanation and trust him that when the time was right and if things progressed with her, he'd expand and tell her everything.

"I get that. I'm going through a lot of changes myself, but it doesn't give me an excuse to be rude to a friend. And I thought we were getting to be friends, Caleb."

Friends was such a bland word when her fresh citrus scent was wafting around him. Her lips still had a light sheen from the gloss she must have put on before she'd headed out.

She shifted again, obliterating the inches of space that

had been between them.

God, he wanted to kiss her. Had wanted to kiss her in her kitchen when they'd flirted over what was in the pastry box. Visions of them sharing the contents had pummeled his brain that day. Her feeding him a morsel and then him returning the favor.

None of those visions had scared him then, unlike seeing her in her exercise clothes with Willow this morning.

Her eyes drifted shut, remained that way for a half a heartbeat, before opening again, drawing him into their gold-brown depths. A flash of pink darted out to moisten her lips. The signs were there that she wanted a kiss as much as he did. And yet he hesitated. He didn't want to be too presumptuous.

The last woman he'd been with had thrown herself at him and he'd taken what she'd given him. They both were aware of what the other could give. Amy had turned out to not be a nice person, but Kerry was becoming important to him in a way a woman hadn't been before.

The timing couldn't be more wrong.

"What are you thinking, Caleb?" she whispered, her hand cupping his cheek.

"I'm thinking I want to kiss you."

A slow, smile worked its way across her face. Her hand against his cheek trailed down until it rested on his shoulder. "Good."

His heart rate skipped up a few notches. "Good?"

"Yes." Kerry shifted her position again and he curled his

arm around her, pulling her tighter against him.

Lowering his head, he arrowed in on his target. The second their lips touched, a sigh rippled through him.

The kiss was light and explorative. Her body melted against him, and he traced the seam of her lips with his tongue. She opened beneath him, deepening the kiss. She tasted faintly of the sparkling grape juice that was being served.

He drew back softly, reluctant to break the connection but not wanting to get too heavy at the same time. This was a first kiss he'd never forget.

Her fingers squeezed his shoulders, once, twice before she leaned in again and placed two soft kisses against his lips. "I should go back in and check on Willow and Dad."

"Yeah, I suppose you should." Kerry hadn't made any moves to extricate from his arms, and he wasn't doing anything to help her. He liked having her close, and he wanted to taste her again.

He lowered his head to hers, but this time instead of a sweet getting-to-know-you kiss, this was deep and carnal.

She practically crawled onto his lap, and he had to tighten his hold on her so she wouldn't fall. Her mouth almost devoured his, and he was happy to let her take the lead. This time their tongues dueled and he ran his hands down her back to her ass, squeezing the firm flesh through her jeans. Her breasts were crushed against his chest, the tight peaks of her nipples brushing against him.

He'd dislodged her shirt and slipped his fingers beneath

the silky fabric to trace the waistline of her jeans. Her skin was warm beneath his touch.

Eventually the need to breathe overcame the need to explore her lips. This time when they parted, she buried her head into his neck, her breath coming in hot pants against his heated skin.

His dick pushed against the confines of his jeans. Moving was going to be difficult for him for a little bit.

With deep reluctance, he lifted her off and placed her back on the seat beside him. In the past, he'd race off to have meaningless sex with any other girl who'd kissed him like that. But not Kerry. When—well, if—they pursued a relationship and ended up in bed together, he wanted it to mean more than any other liaison he'd ever had. And the thought made little sense to him.

The last year had shown him how fragile life could be. How it could be taken in a flash, that loving someone wasn't enough to keep them safe. But he didn't love Kerry, and that was a ridiculous notion to even consider. He hardly knew her.

Still, the kiss they'd shared sparked reactions he hadn't had before. His heart still pounded and his fingers itched to pull her against him. This time, he wanted to take it slow and explore whatever it was growing between them, but it also scared the crap out of him.

He so wasn't ready for this. And he wasn't sure if Kerry was either.

Chapter Eight

THE RESTAURANT WAS buzzing with people and Kerry was doing her best to make sure everything was running smoothly by helping out at the front of the house. It hadn't helped that sleep had been elusive the night before. She touched her lips, imaging Caleb's pressed against them.

"Kerry, Rocco needs to see you. He said it's *urgent*," Leanne, the hostess, said.

Sheesh, she needed to keep her mind on her job. Just the other day the owner of the restaurant had called her in for a special meeting. At the time, she'd been panicking she was about to get fired, but he'd told her he was happy with how she was managing the place and waived the rest of her probation. She was now a full-fledged permanent member of staff.

Relief had been instant, but now that she didn't have that hanging over her head, it didn't mean she had to slack off, because everything could change quicker than a blink of an eye. With her employment secure, she could start a savings account. Have a nest egg to fall back on should she need it. Maybe even plan an overseas vacation. She'd always dreamed of going to Paris.

But not today.

"Let me go see what's wrong." She stood.

"He probably cut a tomato the wrong way," Leanne grumbled under her breath.

Kerry swallowed a laugh and weaved her way through the tables toward the kitchen. Rocco was an emotional chef, but his food was out of this world and every night there was a line of people waiting to get a table.

The rich aroma of garlic, tomatoes, and basil assailed her senses. San Antonio was known for its Mexican cuisine so opening an Italian restaurant was always a risk, but Max, the owner, had taken the plunge and it had paid off. It also helped he'd lured Rocco, now rushing toward her, away from a high-end restaurant in Houston.

"Hey, Chef, what's the problem?"

"Kerry, *ma belle*, you under ordered the salmon. I don't have enough to cover the special tonight."

"What? Let me get the order form you completed. I know I got the required amount off the list."

She rushed out the side door from the kitchen and headed down the hallway to her office. There was no way she under ordered. She *always* triple-checked the order with the suppliers. While the restaurant hadn't been open for long, Rocco's particular reputation had made the rounds around town quicker than a jackrabbit racing away from a pot of boiling water.

She riffled through the colored folders on the desk and picked up the purple one. A minute later she was back in the kitchen. "Okay, here it is." She pulled out two sheets of paper—one was her order and the second was Rocco's order. A quick perusal showed the numbers matched.

Relief flowed through her.

Rocco snatched the papers from her hand. "Hmph. Well, okay. Just tell the staff that the salmon special is now unavailable." He tossed the papers at her and turned back to his station. Kerry caught them up before they hit the floor. As she put them in the folder, she caught the sous chef's eye, who mouthed *thank you* and went back to work.

She guessed that life in the kitchen just got a little better. Triple-checking paid off.

Kerry had just sat down at her chair when a knock sounded on her doorframe. She looked up and saw Leanne standing in the doorway.

"Oh no, what now? Is Rocco still fuming? I just left him."

Leanne laughed lightly. "No, nothing like that. Someone's asking to see the manager."

Her triumphant mood deflated quicker than a balloon. This was her job, one high followed by three lows. She pushed back from her chair. "Okay, which table, and were you aware of any problems before they asked to see me?"

Leanne shook her head. "Trudy just told me that the guy at table fourteen is asking to see the manager. As far as she could remember, she hadn't mucked up their order or drinks."

"Did they want to order the salmon?" she asked. Some people got very annoyed when they found out one of the specials was no longer available.

"Nope. Both he and his date ordered the pasta special."

"Okay, let me see what the issue is." They were almost back into the main seating area when she halted Leanne's progress. "What's the wait time now for a table?"

"What it always is. Twenty minutes."

"You're doing a great job getting the tables turned over in a reasonable time. I know part of our success is due to you."

"Thanks, Kerry, but we're a team, and when you're the manager on duty, everything is always running smoothly. Not to say Jon doesn't do a good job, you just do it better."

Kerry absorbed the praise and let it fortify her for what she was about to find out when she visited table fourteen.

The man at the table in question was facing away from her approach, so she was able to study his date. She was a lovely woman. Her hair curled artfully over her shoulders and her makeup was impeccable. Kerry's own hand wandered toward the neat knot at the nape of her neck before she halted its movement.

Why the hell was she comparing herself to a complete stranger? Beautiful women and handsome men weren't uncommon in the restaurant. But her sixth sense was tingling, and she didn't want to ignore it.

The way the man sat in the chair was familiar to her. Perhaps it was a repeat customer and he wanted to sing the praises of his experience to the management.

She approached the table and pasted a *welcome* smile on her face. "Good evening. My name is Kerry and I'm the manager. You asked to see me?"

Her smile froze into place as her gaze connected with Winthorn Hartigan the third. The last man she ever wanted to see again.

Why the hell was he visiting a restaurant on the River-walk? More to the point, what the hell was he doing in San Antonio? He lived, worked, and socialized in Dallas.

"Well, Kerry, this is a nice surprise and happy coincidence. How are you?"

There was nothing surprising or happy coincidence about this at all. After being in a relationship with the guy for more than seven years, she was well aware that everything Winthorn did was premeditated and very calculated.

"I'm well, thank you. And, yes, this is a surprise." No way was she going to let on that being around him made her uncomfortable. She would rather withstand the tongue-lashings Rocco gave his kitchen helpers than show any sign of weakness around her ex. "Is there a problem you wish to discuss?"

His eyes narrowed, as if he were annoyed she remained calm in his presence. Did he want her to embarrass herself at her job by yelling at him? Or did he want her to crumple into a pile of wet noodles like she'd always done around him and beg him to take her back? Well, he was jack shit out of luck. She had no plans to do any of those things.

"The matter I want to talk to you about, Kerry, is personal. Perhaps we could go somewhere and talk?"

Seriously, he wanted to talk to her about a personal matter when he was on a date? Kerry flicked a glance at his companion. She was busy studying her phone, but her cheeks carried a slight shade of pink.

His date was as uncomfortable with the turn of events as Kerry was.

"I'm afraid unless this *personal matter* is related to the restaurant in some way, it will have to wait." Damn, that felt good. Never before had she had the courage to stand up to Winthorn and go against his edicts. Early in their relationship, she'd answered him back, but over time, without her even being aware of it, her backbone had been whittled away until it was too late.

"It's not a good idea to dismiss me, Kerry." His tone was hard and menacing.

"And I don't appreciate being threatened either. Now, if that's all, I hope you enjoy the rest of your evening." She looked over at his date. "Can I get you another drink, on the house?"

The woman looked up from her phone. "No, thank you." She threw her napkin down on the table and stood. "I think I'll be going, and it's not because of the food or service. It's because of the company."

Kerry bit back a smile at the way Winthorn's date strode toward the exit. If only she'd had that sort of confidence to walk away from him all those years ago. Then she might have really lived. Had a close group of girlfriends to go out with. Decided what she wanted to do for herself, and if it was the wrong thing, well, she lived with the consequences. Instead, she'd had every decision made for her and she wasn't allowed to make her own friends.

"This isn't over, Kerry. I'm not going anywhere. I'm going to be in San Antonio for the next couple of months conducting some business. Mark my words, you'll regret not taking the time to talk to me tonight." He tossed some bills on the table and stomped out.

A breath whooshed out of her, and she reached down to collect the notes, hoping he'd left enough to cover the tip for his server. If not, she'd make sure she did.

"Are you okay, dear?" Kerry turned to look at the couple seated adjacent to the table. Of course the whole restaurant would've witnessed the scene. This was the last thing she and the restaurant needed; a bad Yelp review could kill the buzz that had been created.

"Yes, I am. I apologize for the disruption to your evening. Can I get you anything? Maybe a complementary dessert?"

"Oh, dear, I don't need anything. I'm impressed at how

well you handled that jerk. You were very professional. I'll be telling all my friends to come here. The food is delicious. The service outstanding."

"Thank you very much, ma'am. I appreciate your words, and I know the rest of the staff will too."

"Well, if he was a person from your past, I think you're well rid of him," the lady continued. "Don't have time for people like him." She finished on a sniff of disgust.

Kerry couldn't help but chuckle at the indignation this complete stranger felt on her behalf. "Thank you again. I hope you enjoy the rest of your evening."

All she wanted to do was run back to her office and forget the last fifteen minutes had ever happened. Maybe she'd never have to see Winthorn Hartigan the third, ever again. Unfortunately, she didn't think this particular wish was going to come true. Winthorn was back, and nothing good was going to come of his presence.

THE HOUSE WAS silent when Kerry unlocked the door. The rest of the evening had passed without any more drama, for which she was grateful. Hopefully, the owner wouldn't hear about her run-in with Winthorn in front of the patrons and decide he'd made a huge mistake cutting short her probationary period.

She dumped her purse on the countertop and paused.

Something wasn't right. Willow always greeted her when she walked in.

Quietly, she made her way down the hall to her father's room. Perhaps the door was shut and she was stuck in his room.

Nope. The door stood wide open and Dad was snoring softly.

"Oh no, she didn't, did she?"

Kerry headed toward the back of the house. Was it possible Caleb hadn't locked the doggie door when he left? Nope, the door was locked.

"Where the hell is she?" Willow not coming to greet her was very out of character. Maybe the dog was locked in her bedroom.

As she passed the living room she looked in—and stopped. Lying on the couch was a slumbering Caleb. Willow lay on the ground beside the couch, Caleb's hand resting on her back.

Slipping off her shoes, Kerry padded into the room. The closer she got to the couch, the more obvious it was that something was happening with her neighbor. Sweat beaded his brow and his lips were moving but no sound came out.

He was in the throes of a nightmare.

Willow sat up and Caleb's fingers tightened around her coarse fur. Did she wake Caleb, or did she let him sleep? If she woke him, would he hurt her? She'd read about that happening to some people. Instinctively she knew he'd feel terrible if he did something to her or Willow.

A low moan sounded from him, and he released his hold on Willow and grabbed at his leg. It was the leg he favored when he walked. Willow joined Kerry and hopped on her hind legs, her sign that she wanted to be picked up.

Kerry did and Willow snuggled against her shoulder for a second before pulling away, straining toward the couch.

"No, baby, I don't think that's a good idea," she murmured. Every day, her dog amazed her with her ability to sense another person's sorrow. On this occasion, proceeding with caution was her best option. However, Willow had other ideas and pulled away from her arms so far Kerry almost dropped her. She gave in; hopefully, she wouldn't regret what she was about to do.

She carefully placed Willow in the small gap behind Caleb's curved legs. What Willow would do next was anyone's guess. In all their therapy training and situations, they'd never run through a scenario of someone having a nightmare.

Her dog carefully moved herself into a position where she didn't jostle the sleeping giant and then rested her snout on Caleb's leg while nudging him at the same time. She repeated the action until Caleb jolted awake.

"What?" He sat up, winced, and scrubbed a hand down his face. His gaze locked on hers. "How long have you been there?"

Oh boy, he wasn't happy about finding her standing over

him. He had to recall he'd been having a nightmare.

She couldn't say she'd just walked in. Caleb would be well aware that Willow being on the couch next to him was because of her.

"Um, not long. Are you okay?"

"Fine." The word fired out of him and he swung his legs to the ground. Willow took quick advantage of the added space and sidled up until she could snuggle into his side. Sure, he'd push the dog away. He'd done it so many times in her presence.

When his hand reached out and curved around Willow's head, she relaxed her muscles. "Can I get you some water or something?"

"Yeah, water will be great, thanks."

Kerry rushed out to the kitchen and grabbed a bottle out of the fridge. Her offer was automatic and she'd been surprised he accepted it. On her way back to the living room, she poked her head in her dad's room. He was still snoring away; no doubt the painkillers he still took in the evenings were helping. If all went well at his appointment at the end of the week, Caleb's services would no longer be required.

A stab of disappointment pierced her gut. She pushed the thought aside. It wasn't like she wouldn't see him again. He was her neighbor.

Her lips tingled in remembrance of their kiss. She wouldn't mind experiencing another one.

Geez, she needed to put the halt to these thoughts. She

was getting her life on her own track, no one else's. Getting involved with Caleb was the worst thing she could do.

Willow's barking set Kerry's feet in motion and she rushed back into the living room. When she got there, Caleb's face was contorted in pain and his fingers were digging into his thigh, Willow on her stomach, looking intently at her friend.

"Are you okay?" she asked as she reached his side and held out the bottle. "Do you need painkillers? I can get you some."

"No, I'm fine," he said, his jaw clenched as he grabbed the water from her.

Of course, he would say that. Most guys did. They never wanted to accept that they were in pain. Didn't want to seem to be unmanly.

"Great, so you can make your own way home then?" Whoa, way to be a bitch, but she was pretty sick and tired of macho men.

Willow sat up abruptly and cocked her head. If her dog could talk, Kerry imagined her pet would be telling her, her comments were unwarranted.

Caleb held up his hand in surrender. "Sorry, I'm just…"

"Yeah, I know," she responded quietly. And she did. This guy was a military guy. From what Eric and her father had said, he was going through a major change. What that change was, she had no idea. But clearly he was like some of the people at the veterans' center, suffering from a form of

PTSD. Heck Willow was always picking up on his distress.

He took a few slugs of water from the bottle and silence stretched between them. Willow maintained her position by his side. After a few more minutes, he stood, and she watched him for any signs of distress or pain from his leg. Apart from a slight wince he appeared to be fine.

"I'm sorry for falling asleep on your couch."

She waved away his apology. "It's not a problem. Dad's appointment is at the end of the week so in a few days you'll be able to go back to your normal schedule before we disrupted it."

Caleb looked around the room, at Willow, and then finally rested his gaze on her. "It hasn't been an issue. In fact, I think helping Ron was exactly what I needed in my life. But I will be glad to go back to doing my own thing."

Now that was the last thing she expected to hear from him, admitting that being around Dad was what he wanted. "Well, that's good. I'm sure, if you still feel like you want to, Dad wouldn't mind you visiting him. Even if the doctor clears him to be more mobile, he's not in a position to go back to living by himself."

She willed herself not to squirm beneath his scrutiny. "You like having him here, don't you?"

She shrugged. "Yeah, it's been good having him around. Even though it wasn't expected. I've missed spending time with him."

She hadn't spent as much time with Mom and Dad after

she met Winthorn. Like everything, over time he'd whittled into those visits until they'd been scarce. Of course, moving her to Dallas made it easy for him.

God, how had she been so blind? And why was he here in San Antonio? Sure, he said he was here for work, but he was vice president of his father's firm, He never ventured far from his cushy corner office. Winthorn never acted without a plan, and she would love to know what the plan was and how he thought she fitted into it.

"Is everything okay?" Caleb asked.

Startled, she looked up to find he'd moved to stand beside her. How had she not picked up on that?

Tiredness.

Who was she trying to kid? She'd been sucked into the hole of her past again. That hole was one she didn't plan on falling into again. Regardless of his threats, he wasn't going to bully her anymore.

"I'm just tired," she said. Lame excuse and all, it was one that worked for the moment. "It's been a long night."

Caleb leaned closer, hooking a stray tendril of hair behind her ear. "I should let you go."

"Yeah." But she made no move to distance herself from him.

His fingers lingered at the back of her head and a sigh rippled through her at the connection. Without conscious thought, her eyelids drifted shut and she swayed toward him. When his arms closed around her, a sense of peace flowed through her.

Inhaling, she caught the faint whiff of his citrusy scent, and her arms banded around his waist.

God, she'd forgotten how wonderful it was to be held. What would it be like to come home after a long night at the restaurant and be welcomed with a hug like this?

Bliss, that was what it would be. Only bliss wasn't going to be found with Caleb. Underneath all his hurt, he was a man with a strong personality. She'd been overtaken by one strong man before. She couldn't let it happen to her again. No matter how much she might think she wanted it with him.

Chapter Nine

THE NEXT MORNING, Caleb stared out the kitchen window at his back yard, cleaning his coffeepot.

Falling asleep on Kerry's couch hadn't been his plan at all. He'd intended to go home after Ron went to bed. Except that plan had gone awry and he'd ended up having a nightmare and Kerry witnessed it all. Not that she let on that she'd seen him in the throes of him reliving the worst day of his life, but he'd seen the sympathy and pity in her eyes.

Thank goodness he could now go back to his normal routine soon. Only the thought of staying home alone didn't appeal anymore. For the first time in a long time, he'd begun to think of what he could do with his future. He could be medically discharged with his benefits. Or he could see what other options were available to him after the medical board made its final ruling. It was time he headed to the base and spoke to his superior officer.

What he was going to do after he made his final decision, he had no idea, but maybe talking to Lieutenant Colonial Blue would give him some clarity. Or he could talk to people at the veterans' center.

He couldn't deny he'd had a good time there. It hadn't hurt as much as he thought it would to be around ex-military personnel. The guys he'd talked to were open with their pain and how they'd adjusted to life after a career in the armed forces.

He made to shift away from the window when he noticed movement in the far back corner of his yard. He leaned forward in an attempt to get a closer look, which was stupid, as the distance hadn't reduced between his location and the object.

As he watched, a little face appeared, followed by a short, squat body.

"Well, I'll be damned." He chuckled when Willow waddled her way across his yard. Now that he knew where she was getting in, he'd be able to fix it so she couldn't escape into his yard.

No sooner had he finished the thought than he banished it. Over the past few weeks, the little dog had grown on him.

Keeping his distance from dogs would be impossible if he stayed in the military thanks to his years of association and years of service in the K-9 unit. He would've still been around them on base. A transfer to another base was possible but, despite the heat, humidity, and lack of real seasons, he liked living in San Antonio. It was a vibrant city and he couldn't deny the Tex-Mex was pretty awesome. If the ruling meant he had to leave the air force, he'd have to find something to do.

Never in his life had he rested on his laurels and he wasn't planning to start now, even if he'd spent the almost twelve months merely existing instead of living.

Pushing away from the kitchen counter, he made his way to his back door, opening it to find Willow sitting by the door, her little face smiling up at him.

"What are you doing here, young lady?" Her tail wagged in response. Chuckling, he bent down and picked her up. Her warm body snuggled into his chest. He breathed deeply and scrunched up his nose. "Geez, dog, you need a bath."

She made a snuffling sound as if she agreed. "Don't look at me, girlie, I'm not your owner. And speaking of your owner, I'm sure she's worried about you."

Slipping into his slides, he juggled the dog and grabbed his keys off the hook. Locking up his house, he strode down his front path, heading for Kerry's house.

He raised his fist to knock when the door opened abruptly. "Oh God, Caleb, I'm so sorry. I don't know how she got out again. I was outside with her, but I turned my back to straighten some potted plants and then when I looked back, she'd disappeared again."

"It's fine. I was up, so she didn't bother me. I found out where she came through too."

"You did? Where? I looked everywhere and couldn't find anything."

"I know; I did too. She gets through right in the far corner of the yard where the side fence meets the back fence. I'll fix it up."

Kerry shook her head, exasperation written on her face. "I looked there and couldn't see anything. She's a damn Houdini, that's what she is."

He hoisted Willow a little higher in his arms. "She's wily and determined, that's for sure. Must take after her owner."

A pink hue swept up Kerry's face. "Thank you. Let me take her from you." She held out her arms, and he took in the spaghetti strap pink tank and matching sleep shorts she was wearing. The fabric clung to her breasts, her nipples protruding through the thin material. He could picture his hands cupping her pert breasts while her legs wrapped around him as he drove into her.

His cock immediately hardened against his sweatpants.

Fuck, it had been a long time since he'd had this type of visceral response to a woman. A woman he'd only kissed once.

Caleb tightened his hold on Willow. He willed his body to settle the hell down as well. If he handed Willow over, there was no way he could hide his body's reaction.

"I can bring her inside if you'd like." Her eyebrow quirked at his comment. "Or I can put her down or give her to you. Whatever," he tacked on quickly.

Man, what the hell was wrong with him? She probably thought he'd lost his mind. And perhaps he had.

"Umm. Yeah, if you want."

Now she sounded confused. He shifted his gaze from the

paint chipping on the doorframe to the left of her shoulder to study her a little more. The faint pink hue had blossomed into a darker tone on her cheeks and her fingers were gripping the door so the whites of her knuckles showed. Her breathing hitched up a couple of notches and her eyes kept straying to his chest.

His cock twitched again, getting the message quicker than his brain.

Her tongue darted out to wet her lips, and he groaned inwardly. She was going to kill him without even using a weapon.

For years, he'd been an action man, had to be with his job. Now he was going to throw caution to the wind and take what he wanted, and what he wanted was to kiss Kerry.

Willow wiggled in his arms, and he automatically squatted to put her on the ground. In a flash he was up and he closed the distance between him and Kerry. He didn't care if she could feel how turned-on he was.

"Good morning, Kerry," he murmured before lowering his head and brushing his lips against hers.

"Morning, Caleb," she responded and thrust her fingers into his hair, tugging his head toward hers.

Okay, then, she was on board with an early morning kiss.

He tightened his hold around her waist so their bodies were aligned. His hard dick squashed against her belly was a sensation he enjoyed. The low moan in the back of her throat spurred him to deepen the kiss. Her mouth opened beneath his, and their tongues met in a slow dance.

He traced his fingers down her spine until he found the hem of her short top. Sliding them beneath the cotton, he caressed her back.

The need to sweep her up in his arms and march to her bedroom where he could feast on her delectable breasts and explore the sweetness between her legs threatened to drown him. But part of his brain was aware of their location, and he reluctantly pulled his lips away from hers.

Their breathing sounded harsh against his ears.

"Wow, that was quite the good morning," she said, her lips brushing his ear, and he couldn't stop his full body shudder if he tried.

"Yes, it was." He took a step back but didn't release her completely. He wasn't ready to break their connection.

Willow barked; over Kerry's shoulder he could see her sitting on her haunches, her tongue lolling out of her mouth. He couldn't deny she was a cute little thing, and part of the coldness that had engulfed him the second he'd woken up in a hospital to find out that Trigger was gone dissipated a little.

"What are you doing today?" he asked her, hoping that she didn't have to go to the restaurant until later and she wasn't needed at the veterans' center. Today he wanted her to be near. A feeling he didn't understand.

"I have to be at the restaurant at nine. This week I'm on

during lunch. I should be home around three or four."

"Do you want to go out for dinner?" The invitation burst out of him before he'd really thought things through.

A slow smile broke out over the plump lips he'd just devoured, tempting him to take them again.

"I'd like that," she said, her voice a husky whisper. "I'll have to work something out for Dad, but yes. Yes, I would like to have dinner with you, Caleb."

A sudden cough broke the moment. "Don't worry about me, I'll be fine. I'll call Eric."

Caleb would've pushed Kerry away, but the evidence of how much he desired Ron's daughter was plain to see and he didn't feel like sharing that with the man just yet. Although he had no idea if Ron had seen them kissing. But by the smile on his face, Caleb would hazard a guess that he'd gotten an eyeful.

Kerry wiggled in his hold, so he loosened his arms and let her slip out. He might want to save himself from embarrassment, but no way would he hold a woman against her will.

"Dad, umm, what are you... Okay, sure, that's great. Excuse me." She moved down the hallway, scooping up Willow as she went.

He couldn't help tracking her movement, watching the gentle sway of her hips and her legs showcased in her sleep shorts.

"That's my daughter you're ogling there, young man." Ron's voice might have been stern, but Caleb could see a hint of acceptance in his gaze.

"Sorry, sir." Now he did feel like a teenager. It had been a long time since he'd been chastised for checking out a woman.

Ron beckoned him. Caleb couldn't very well ignore the man in his own home.

"Yes, sir?" he asked when was about a foot away from him.

"Enough with the *sir*, Caleb. We've long passed that formality in our association, I mean, you've had to help me out in some pretty personal situations. But…"

Here it is. What Ron said was the truth; they had shared things most people didn't share. "But?"

"Kerry is my daughter and she's very precious to me. I don't know what she's told you about her past, and it's not my place to inform you, but she was hurt pretty badly and lost herself for a while. I don't want to see that happen to her again. I may be incapacitated at the moment, but if you hurt her, I'll hurt you."

Caleb had no doubt the other man would follow through on his threat if he saw reason to.

"I'll do my best not to hurt her." It was the only thing he could say. Life didn't come with guarantees and he wasn't one to give them out either.

Did that make him a bad person? Possibly, but he preferred to think of himself as a realist. He'd seen enough situations during his deployments that didn't turn out the way people hoped they would.

Hell, he was on US soil when his life had been turned upside down.

"I know you have your own demons to deal with and I'll take your word. But she's my daughter. She's all I have left and I won't lose her again."

Any chance for him to question Ron further was lost when Kerry wandered down the hallway toward them.

"Why are you both still in the hallway?"

She'd put on yoga pants and a T-shirt. He lamented the loss of seeing her sexy legs, but couldn't blame her. "I was just getting ready to leave. I'll be back in an hour and then we can talk about where to go for our da—dinner."

"Sounds good." She walked over to her dad. "Come on, Dad, let's get you some breakfast. You'll be able to see yourself out, right, Caleb?" She gripped her father's wheelchair.

"Sure, I'll be in touch."

"Sounds good." She took two steps then turned to look back at him. The small smile he was beginning to long for when he saw her, tugged at the corners of her mouth. "I'm looking forward to our da—dinner." She winked, and he couldn't help but laugh at her mimicking him.

Lightness filled him as he walked out the door.

Chapter Ten

BUTTERFLIES THE SIZE of Willow's favorite ball filled Kerry's stomach. Why the hell was she so nervous? It was just dinner. Not a date. Caleb's avoidance of the word had ensured she got the message.

They were just two friends going out to dinner. If she had her way, she'd pay for the meal as a way to say thanks for all the help he'd given her over the last few weeks. He'd refused to take any form of payment, said he just wanted to help out.

Who did that? Who looked after a complete stranger out of the goodness of their heart?

Caleb Bradshaw, that was who.

She still didn't understand why he did it. According to her conversations with Eric at the veterans' center, Caleb had been keeping to himself, only going to rehab and then out to some social events when Ethan encouraged him to. Eric didn't mention Caleb's dating life and she didn't ask, although she couldn't deny her curiosity had been piqued.

Giving herself one last look in the mirror, she caught Willow's reflection. "What do you think, Will? Do I pass?"

She did a little twirl, and the skirt of her sky-blue sundress flared out before settling around her legs.

Willow barked and wagged her stumpy tail. "I'll take it as a sign you approve. And I really am losing my mind talking to a dog."

"You look beautiful, sweetie. Caleb is going to be knocked over by your vibrancy."

Her cheeks heated at the compliment. "You're supposed to say things like that because you're my dad, but thank you."

He wheeled himself into her room, stopped in front of her and leaned forward, holding out his hand. She grasped it with both of hers.

"I mean it, Kerry. You look radiant. I haven't seen you looking this happy for a long time. That Hartigan jerk did a number on you. I wish I'd been able to see what was really going on."

Kerry squatted down in front of her father. "Dad, it's okay. I didn't even know what was happening to me until I was out of it and had the distance to see how toxic and abusive our relationship was. It's not your fault, and I don't blame you. When I needed you, you and Mom were there. I just—" She clamped her lips shut, not wanting to express the thoughts that trailed around her mind on occasion.

"Just what? Come on, sweetie, you know you can tell me anything and I won't judge."

She kept her gaze fixed on their clasped hands, not wanting to see the disappointment in his eyes. "It's just, I feel like I disappointed Mom when she learned that Winthorn and I broke up. She liked him a lot and was glad that I was seeing a man who could provide for me."

Dad patted her hand. "Look at me, love," he said quietly.

Taking a deep breath, she lifted her gaze and tears gathered in her eyes. His love for her was shining from his blue depths.

"Kerry, I loved your mother with every fiber of my being. I miss her every day, but her views on life and how you should live yours were very old-fashioned, and in today's current climate, would be looked down on by everyone. She believed you should be looked after so you didn't have to worry about the financial aspect of a relationship. Perhaps that's my fault; whenever I tried to talk to her about money, she always said it was my job and she trusted me. It was an honor that she placed that much trust in me, but it came with a burden too."

"A burden how?"

"Well, when we hit a rough patch with my construction company I couldn't share the troubles with her because I didn't want to worry her. So I carried the load and continued on my way. If she could've really seen how much you'd changed, how much Winthorn had influenced your life, she wouldn't have been happy. But with her illness and knowing she'd not see you get married or have children, she saw what she wanted to see. And that was you in a settled relationship."

Everything her father had just said whirled in Kerry's mind like a mini tornado. Her mom's actions made more sense now, but she still couldn't quite dissolve one small fact.

"But Winthorn and I ended before she died, Dad. That had to have distressed her."

"Kerry, she was in pain at the end and not really aware of what was going on around her. She probably forgot you'd even told her about the breakup. But, sweetie"—he squeezed her hands—"your mom loved you unconditionally. She wouldn't have been disappointed—she'd have been happy that you got yourself out of a horrid situation."

Kerry sniffled and willed the tears in her eyes not to fall. She didn't have time to redo her makeup. "But I didn't get myself out of it. Winthorn pushed me out. If he hadn't, I'd still be in my little bubble, not aware of anything."

"Don't sell yourself short. You'd have worked it out. I know you would have."

Kerry was glad her father had faith in her, because she didn't. Even now, she couldn't help but wonder what her life would've been like if Winthorn hadn't dumped her.

The doorbell rang and Willow barked enthusiastically while she jumped up and down on her stump legs, as high as the bed would let her.

"Kerry, Caleb may have some demons—it's expected after what he must have seen while serving our country—but I believe he's a good guy. He's not Winthorn. He won't try to make you something you're not."

Standing, she scooped Willow from the bed. "I know, Dad. It's just dinner. Not even a date."

Dad laughed. "Right, and I'm not stuck in a wheelchair with two broken legs. Go let him in. Eric said he'd be here in about a half an hour."

"Okay, I'm glad he could come over," she said on her way out the door. She placed Willow on the ground, and she scampered toward the front door. "This dog is 100 percent in love with Caleb."

"She's got good taste. As I said, he's a good guy."

Kerry rolled her eyes, but she couldn't help but agree with his sentiments. Caleb was a good guy.

THEY WALKED PAST the restaurant where she worked, and Leanne, the hostess, waved at her. She waved back, stifling a laugh when she spied the hostess fanning herself after pointing to Caleb.

"You know her?" the man of the hour asked.

"Yeah, that's my restaurant."

Caleb paused, turned around, and studied the restaurant's façade. "*Mia Tesoro*. I've heard of this place."

"Really, what have you heard?" She placed her hand behind her back, crossing her fingers that he'd heard good things about the restaurant.

Caleb took hold of her hand and leaned close. Goose bumps pebbled over her skin. "I've heard"—he paused and she could hit him for giving it a dramatic twist—"it has an excellent reputation, and one of the managers is super efficient and easy on the eyes."

Kerry laughed. "Yes, Jon the manager is very easy on the eyes. Not to mention, as you said, extremely efficient."

"I think you're teasing me," he returned after a couple of heartbeats of silence.

"Yes and no. Jon is a good manager, we work well together. He's also a happily married forty-three-year-old man with three kids."

"Good to know. I still maintain the other manager is very easy on the eyes."

Heat suffused her face, pleased at his compliment. They continued on their way to the steakhouse on the Riverwalk that they'd decided to eat at.

"Here we are?"

A few minutes later they were seated at a table in the upstairs portion of the restaurant overlooking the river.

Why was she so nervous? It wasn't like they hadn't spent time alone together. Although to be fair, Willow had always been around and her dad had been in the other room.

This nondate was really beginning to feel like a date.

"Good evening. My name is Lisa and I'll be your server. Can I get you something to drink?" A rush of relief tempered the butterflies fluttering in her belly.

"Yes, I'll have a glass of the house semillon," Kerry said.

"I'll have a glass of lemonade, please."

"Certainly, I'll be back to take your orders momentarily."

"Didn't pick you for a lemonade type of guy. Tea maybe, beer definitely."

Caleb picked at the top of the napkin his utensils were wrapped in. "I try to avoid alcohol as much as possible."

Kerry mentally kicked herself for her rash comment. One would think that after all the time she'd put in with Willow helping returning servicemen she wouldn't ask something so insensitive. She reached out and placed her hand over his where it rested on the table. "I'm sorry, Caleb, that was thoughtless of me."

He turned his hand over and entwined his fingers with hers and her panic subsided. "I accept your apology. I almost fell into the black alcohol pit after my accident, but I found the strength to grasp the edges and haul my ass out of it."

This was the first time he'd made reference to his accident with her. The accident that was, no doubt, the reason for his limp. No matter how curious she was about it all, she wouldn't question him.

Hell, she had things she didn't want to talk about. Everyone kept parts of themselves hidden. Though what she kept hidden wouldn't be as heroic as Caleb's.

"I'm sorry again for bringing it up. But I'm glad you didn't fall down the pit. So many do. This is why I take Willow down to the center. I know she helps everyone she encounters. And I knew the second I saw her at the rescue home that she was the dog for me."

"You rescued Willow? You haven't had her from a pup?"

With her free hand she drew circles over the top of Caleb's hand, pleased he didn't pull away from her touch. "She was about four months old when I got her so, yeah, she was a pup. But she had the sweetest nature, and I needed that. I've only had her for about a year, and I've been training her since she was six months old."

The waitress returned with their drinks, and they both sat back, breaking the connection between them. They placed their order, but the closeness that had sprung up between them seemed to have disappeared.

"The service—"

"Do you—"

Kerry laughed. "You first," she said and reached for her wine and took a fortifying sip.

"I was going to ask if, when you go out to a restaurant now, do you look more closely at the service and food, or do you switch off and just enjoy the evening?"

She caught a drop of condensation before it dripped to the cloth. "Well, seeing as this is my first dinner since I started working at Mia Tesoro and I haven't worked in a restaurant until now, I can't say what I'll do. But I think I'd like to switch off and enjoy my meal. Whether that will happen or not, only time will tell."

"Where did you used to work before?"

She looked out the window before turning back to him. "This is my first full-time job."

"Really? What did you do before?"

Their meals arrived, halting their conversation, and for that she was grateful. How did she explain she was a thirty-year-old woman who was only just starting her first full-time job? Shame dulled her appetite even though the food smelled delicious.

"Is everything okay?"

"What?"

"You're looking at your food like there's something wrong with it. Do you want me to call the server back?"

Kerry gave herself a mental shake. She was having dinner with a really nice guy. A guy whose kisses curled her toes. She wasn't going to let thoughts of her prior life bring her down any further. "No, everything's fine. I was just thinking about something. Doesn't matter."

She picked up her utensils and cut into the steak. The knife slid through it as though it were butter. A burst of pepper exploded on her tongue with the first bite. The meat was cooked to perfection and, even though she said she wasn't going to, she couldn't help but compare it to Chef Rocco's steak dish at her restaurant. Her meal was just as good as Rocco's. "Wow, this is amazing. How's yours?" she asked.

His fork was midway to his mouth, and desire darkened his already dark eyes. An answering heat filled her. She picked up her glass of water, hoping it was still cold enough to douse the fire burning in her.

She didn't take her eyes off him as she took a long swallow. His Adam's apple mimicked her action.

For endless seconds they stared at each other. She was sure anyone looking at them would be laughing. Her glass was raised and so was his fork, but it was like they'd both been frozen, unable to move.

"Is everything okay with your meals?" Once again, the waitress broke the spell encasing them both.

Kerry smiled up at her. "Yes, it's delicious, thank you."

Caleb grunted. Lisa bestowed a smile and, with an *if you need anything else* edict, left to attend to one of her other tables.

The next few minutes they didn't say anything, just concentrated on eating their food. It also gave Kerry time to get her emotions under control. This wasn't supposed to be happening to her now. Her life was her own. She was in total charge of what she did. How she thought. Whether she wanted to splurge on a new wardrobe or donate a considerable amount to the therapy facility that had trained Willow. All things that had been stolen from her. She had no desire to let herself fall into the trap of being blinded by a man and thinking his actions came from a place of love. For years, she'd thought Winthorn loved her, and, well, maybe in the start he had, but it had turned on her in a way she never imagined love could.

"Is something else wrong with your food?" Caleb asked.

"What? No, it's fine, why?"

"You've been staring off into space for the last few minutes."

God, how could she be so flaky? Her ex should be the last person on her mind while she was out with another man. Part of her worried he would make good on his threat that things weren't over between them.

For her, it definitely was.

Placing her utensils on her plate, she attempted to smile. "Sorry, I was just thinking about something that happened at work last night."

"Wanna talk about it?" Caleb leaned forward, the tips of his fingers meeting hers where they rested on the table. The small connection sent spirals of awareness twirling through her.

"Not really, but thank you for the offer."

"Okay." He sat back, taking his hand with him, and she mourned the loss of his touch. But maybe it was just as well. She couldn't let herself fall into the trap of letting her feelings rule her life again. "You never did tell me how come you're just starting your first job."

Damn, she'd hoped he'd forgotten about his earlier question. She'd tried not to think about it. Lost in the moment of enjoying good food with a very sexy man Caleb, with his rough around the edges loner vibe, had every woman in the room sparing him glances.

"I dropped out of college my last semester and…" She picked up her glass of wine again, draining the remaining contents. "Well, let's just say I made a bad decision and it took me a long time to work out just how bad. But now I've got my degree and I'm working in a job I love, even though it can be tiring. I'm very happy with my life at the moment."

He looked like he wanted to question her more. The night was too special to be ruined by talk of her past.

Please, Caleb. No more questions, leave the subject alone.

"Well, I'm glad you're happy and doing what you love. Not everyone is that lucky."

Was the accident he alluded to earlier the reason for the sadness in his voice? "What do you do in the air force?" she asked, broaching the subject she'd told herself she wouldn't.

"I don't want to talk about it," he said abruptly. His face was like a piece of granite. "You ready to go?"

"Umm, sure, let me just run to the restroom." She picked up her purse without waiting for a response.

Somehow the evening had gone from full of promise to a disaster waiting to happen. Perhaps it was for the best that they called the evening over. Like her, he had secrets he didn't want to share. She should respect it, but why did it hurt so much?

Chapter Eleven

THE WALK BACK to the car was filled with tension. Caleb was well aware he was responsible for it. He shouldn't have snapped at Kerry when she asked him about what he did for a living. She'd answered his questions, shared a part of her he could see was hard to share.

It still intrigued him what the backstory was for the delay in getting a job. Perhaps she'd been married and she hadn't needed to work. Ron had said she'd been hurt in the past. That could mean many things. Maybe her husband had died recently and it hurt too much to talk about him. But there were no wedding photos on her mantel or pictures of her with a man. During his time in the armed services, he'd been to widows' houses and they still had pictures of their fallen husbands on display, even if they'd moved on and remarried. Plus, he was sure Ron would've mentioned a former son-in-law. Or maybe she'd been through an acrimonious divorce and neither of them wanted to talk about it to him.

Although, now that he thought about it, they hadn't touched on Kerry's past all that much. He hadn't wanted to seem too interested, and Ron was clearly protecting his daughter's privacy.

Still, he'd been an asshole when he had no reason to be, and their evening had been going so well. He'd been having the best time he'd had in a long while. Sitting across the table from Kerry had highlighted just how off track he'd gotten with the women he'd dated since his accident.

"I worked in the K-9 division," he said, shattering the silence that engulfed them.

"Pardon?" Kerry asked, stopping, her eyebrows drawn together in confusion.

"Back in the restaurant, you asked me what I did and I brushed you off. Actually, I was very rude. And I'm sorry for that."

The confusion cleared from her face, but there was still a hint of wariness in her eyes, a shadow suggesting she'd heard apologies before but then they'd been retracted with the next break.

"Thank you." She continued walking away.

He'd well and truly fucked this up.

He should fix it. He should stop her and make her understand a little of why he was feeling the way he did about his job.

Yet he hesitated. Perhaps it was for the best that this night be a one-off thing for the two of them. Until he had his life sorted out, was he really in a position to embark on a relationship with a woman?

Relationship.

Where had that thought come from? At a few months shy of thirty-eight, most of the guys he associated with were married with kids or at the very least in serious relationships. Hell, some had divorced and remarried. His former roommate's fiancée had been married to a military man who died in a training exercise and now she was taking the plunge again. People leaped when their life was in turmoil, found the arms of a loved one who helped them through whatever tragedy they were going through.

Why couldn't he?

Why couldn't he lay his troubles down in front of Kerry?

Fear.

Plain and simple fear. Why else had he taken up with women who weren't looking for a long-term future with him? Hell, Amy, the last woman he'd been seeing, was having one last fling before settling down with the man her family had lined up for her to marry. But then she'd clung on longer than Caleb thought she would, and it had been difficult to extricate from her.

Kerry had continued walking, and if he wasn't careful, he was going to lose her in the crowd of people around the Riverwalk. He set off after her at a quick pace, ignoring the sting in his leg.

"Kerry, wait!" Relief pounded through him when she stopped.

"Yes?"

Okay, so she wasn't going to give him an inch, and he

supposed he deserved it. "Look, I know I shouldn't have reacted the way I did in the restaurant when you questioned me. Talking about my career is hard at the moment."

"And you think blurting out that at thirty I'm just starting my first job was easy? I thought we were at least friends, Caleb, and friends share stuff."

"We are friends, Kerry. We are." Unfortunately, the light and happiness he usually spied in her eyes was missing.

"Well, I'm not so sure." Her shoulders slumped, and he wanted to pull her into his arms and kiss away the sorrow. Yeah, he didn't think she would appreciate it.

"What can I do?" he asked.

"Take me home. I think it's probably best we go back to the way things were before tonight. Heck, before this morning when you kissed me. You're helping me out with my dad, which I really appreciate, so we should leave it at that. The job could be finished in a couple days when Dad goes to the doctor and we can go back to being just neighbors."

Her arms were crossed over her chest, her pose as defensive as a row of airmen with their guns raised. Her chin lifted, daring him to object.

The last thing he wanted to do was force her into something she didn't want, even though he suspected deep down this reaction was coming purely from a place of hurt, not from any dislike for him. Well, he hoped that was the case.

Earlier when he'd watched her eat, and their eyes had

connected and held, she couldn't have faked her reaction. She liked and wanted him just as much as he liked and wanted her. What he had to do was come at this strategically.

Because, dammit, Kerry was good for him and he liked to think he was good for her too. He just had to find out a way to convince her.

KERRY WAS DOING a bang-up job of avoiding him. As she'd predicted at their dinner, the doctor had removed the cast on Ron's right leg, giving him more freedom with the ability to get around on his crutches. Even Willow hadn't turned up in his yard unannounced. He hadn't fixed the area of the fence, even though he'd told Kerry he would. Admitting that Willow had grown on him had all been part of the adjustment he'd gone through mentally.

Caleb checked his appearance in the mirror one last time. Before he met with his lieutenant colonel in a few days to discuss his future, he intended to speak to Kerry, see if they could start over.

First though, he had to see if she was home and wanted to take Willow for a walk.

Okay, he couldn't put it off any longer. He snatched up his keys, pulled his door open, and stepped out into the Texas sunshine. The humidity in the air left his clothes clinging to him after two strides.

When he reached Kerry's front door, he took a moment to center his thoughts then raised his fist to knock.

"Coming," Ron's voice filtered through the wood. He strained to see if he could hear the telltale clipping of Willow's nails. Of course, that was ridiculous considering it was thick wood.

Ron's face brightened after he opened the door.

"Hey, Ron, is it okay if I come in?"

"Sure, sure. Hang on, let me get out of the way. Damn crutches, it should be easier now that I only have one leg in a cast, but I'm still hopeless."

No matter how hard he tried, Caleb couldn't prevent the smile from breaking out over his face as he watched Ron hop and shift awkwardly. "By this time tomorrow, you'll be a whiz on those things."

"I think the wheelchair was easier to deal with, even though I hated being in it."

"Maybe you should look at getting one of those one-leg scooters," Caleb suggested as he walked into the hallway, closing the door behind him. A cool breeze from the air conditioning flowed over him. He closed his eyes and stood there for a few seconds, savoring being able to feel cool again.

"Funny you should say that. Kerry's going to speak to someone while she's at the veterans' center today about it."

Disappointment flared through him. But he already knew she was gone when he hadn't spied Willow's happy face. "Oh well, that's good. I take it Kerry's not here?" He tried to keep his voice as neutral as possible. Ron raised his eyebrow—clearly Caleb hadn't succeeded.

"No. Did you want to see her?"

Caleb sighed. He could lie to Ron and say he was here to see him, but he wasn't that type of person and Ron wouldn't appreciate it either. "Yeah, I was hoping to."

Ron seated himself in his chair and let out a groan. "I really hope she comes home with a scooter. I thought I'd like being on crutches and independent, but it's harder than I thought it was going to be."

"Do you need something? You know you can call me and I'll come and help you out."

Ron sat quietly for a few moments, watching him. The action reminded Caleb of sitting opposite his superior officer, waiting for him to take Caleb to task for an error he'd made while training or on deployment. Like he did in those situations, Caleb straightened his spine and met the other man's gaze head-on. No matter what Kerry's dad said, he'd accept it and move on, even if it was a *leave my daughter the hell alone* lecture.

"I wasn't sure you'd want to, considering you seemed eager to be as far away from here as possible. Today's the first day since we came back from the doctor's that you've bothered to show up."

Caleb scrubbed a hand down his face. He couldn't fault Ron; he had kept his distance. "Yeah, I know. I'm sorry. I've had to do a little thinking about what I'm going to do and where my life is headed. It's been off track for a while."

"And what have you decided?"

Well, that was getting straight to the point, wasn't it? "In certain aspects, I'm still wavering, and in others, yeah, I think I do."

"And does Kerry fit in with any of this?"

How did he answer this without putting his main ally offside? There was a spark between them that she felt as much as he did. So he would do everything he could to change her mind. But regardless of what he wanted, if she made it clear she wanted nothing to do with him, he'd walk.

"Well, sir, that's up to your daughter. I've discovered that I like her and enjoy being with her, and I want to explore that. If she doesn't, well then, I'll leave her be."

Ron studied him, as if trying to determine whether he was talking truth or bullshit. Over the time they'd spent together, he'd been honest with Ron. Sure, he might not have told him about his accident and Trigger's death. Talking about that was hard. Without a doubt he'd have to explain it all to Kerry if he wanted a future with her. That was, if he found her and she was willing to talk to him.

"My daughter is all I have left, and I've loved her from the second my late wife told me she was expecting. I'll do anything to protect her. I'm not going to go into details, because, as I mentioned, it's not my story tell. But let me reiterate. She's been hurt in the past and, well, I don't want to see that happen to her again."

Caleb got the message loud and clear. "Understood."

"She'll be at the veterans' center for a little longer. If you're interested."

Oh, he was very interested. He smiled. He'd been granted permission he hadn't known he'd been seeking. Kerry—well, she was special and he wanted to do everything right when it came to her.

Chapter Twelve

KERRY SMILED AT George as he placed the folded leg scooter in her trunk. "Thanks, George. Dad is going to appreciate having this. He just can't get the hang of crutches. I thought his awkwardness was because of having both legs in casts, but it's not. He's just not crutch coordinated."

The older man laughed and slammed the trunk shut. "Yeah, crutches can be a bitch to deal with, especially if you have stairs in the house."

"Well, thank goodness, I don't have stairs," Kerry commented as they walked back into the building.

"Willow's been a real help to a lot of the guys here. I hope you know how much we appreciate the time you take out of the day to bring her down." George, a former Vietnam veteran, was the director of the center. He'd put a call out for a therapy dog just as she had completed Willow's training, so Kerry had jumped at the chance to put all they'd learned into practice.

She couldn't describe the emotions that had bubbled inside of her when she'd seen Willow help her first person. Now she wished she could do more, but she needed her job to pay for her house.

"We love coming here, George. It's crazy. Willow seems to know which days we're coming because she's whimpering with excitement in the car when we get about a quarter mile from here. If I didn't have her in a doggie seat in the back of the car, she'd leap out the second I opened the door. And, as you know, that's not the easiest thing for a corgi to do."

George laughed as they walked back into the coolness of the building. "Now that's a sight I wouldn't mind seeing. But so long as she doesn't hurt herself, of course. We'd be lost without our Willow here."

Pride at her dog burst within her. Never in a million years would she have ever thought she'd volunteer at a veterans' center. For sure, if she'd still been with Winthorn, he wouldn't have allowed her to do it. Of course, he wouldn't have allowed her to have a dog. Or anything that took her attention away from him.

God, why was she *still* thinking about the jerk? Since her run-in with him at the restaurant, she hadn't heard a peep from him so his threat to her had been as empty as his heart.

"I'll speak to you later, Kerry. Let me know if your dad needs anything else, and also let him know he's welcome here anytime. The other guys enjoy his company."

"Thanks, George, I'll tell him. He'll get a buzz out of hearing that. He enjoys coming here too. Since Mom died, he's been trying to find something that fulfills his time—hence he thought skiing might be something he could take up. Visiting here is a much safer venture. Not to mention he enjoys playing cards with Eric and the others."

George laughed as he headed down the hallway to his office. Kerry couldn't deny the place was therapeutic for her as well. Over the last week, she'd been able to keep her thoughts of Caleb to a bare minimum when she and Willow were here doing their job. Which was strange considering the company she was keeping. Being surrounded by military personnel should've brought Caleb front and center in her mind, and she couldn't deny that if she let herself, she'd imagine him standing in the doorway of the game room, like she was doing right now.

She closed her eyes and shook her head. Imagining Caleb standing in this building was crazy. She'd gone out of her way to make sure she wasn't in his orbit after their date. And he'd done the same.

Once she was sure thoughts of Caleb had cleared her mind, she opened her eyes, her gaze tracking to the spot where she'd imagined he was standing. But instead of the doorway being empty, there he was, still standing there, although he wasn't peering into the room like he had when she'd first spied him. No, his eyes were on her, pinning her to the spot.

He straightened his stance and she willed her legs to move. It wasn't like she could go home, because Willow was still on duty. But she could pretend she needed the bathroom or wanted a drink or something instead of standing there like a statute.

Ever since Caleb entered her orbit, she'd been drawn to him like a moth to a flame. But past experience had taught her that was the first step on the road to hell. She'd sworn that no way would she let a guy dictate her every move, and so far, she'd stayed strong and kept that oath. Not that being around Caleb had ever made her feel weak.

If anyone would be hell-bent on controlling situations around him, it would be Caleb. He was in the air force. He walked into dangerous situations all the time. She'd done a little bit of research about the K-9 division. They were in first, checking to make sure the building was free of explosives or hunting for the insurgent they were after.

Of course, he'd want to be in control of all aspects of his life, including a relationship.

Regardless of all those thoughts, the time had come to be truthful and admit she'd missed him. Missed seeing him sitting in the corner of her couch, legs stretched out in front of him, one ankle crossed over the other. His hair was never as neatly combed as it looked now with him standing right in front of her. At this moment, all she wanted to do was run toward him and have his strong arms wrap around her.

"Hi, Kerry." A small smile teased his lips and the citrusy scent he always wore wafted around her. It took everything in her not to sway. The scent was intoxicating; whenever she smelled oranges at the grocery store her thoughts invariably tracked to him.

"Hi, Caleb, what are you doing here?" Excellent, her voice sounded strong and sure, like having him close wasn't affecting her at all. Of course, her heart was beating out of her chest.

"I came to see you."

Well, that was the last thing she'd expected to hear from him. He'd done everything possible to avoid being around her since their date.

And you didn't?

Damn that little voice in her head. Yes, she'd avoided seeing him too. It would be easy to make excuses for the way she'd acted. All of them valid in her mind, yet kind of petty at the same time.

"Why did you come to see me here? You could've come to my house anytime you wanted."

Her voice rose a little, and she became conscious of some of the occupants of the room looking at them. The last thing she wanted was to become a spectacle in front of the people she came to help.

"I dropped by your place this morning. You weren't there, and this is where Ron said you'd be." Caleb kept his voice low and modulated, as if he didn't want to create a scene either.

Her heart warmed a little. He'd made the first move. Now it was up to her to either take it or push it away—and pushing it away was the last thing she wanted. "I… uh, I should be finished here in an hour. We can go for a walk after and talk if you want."

Caleb smiled, the corners of his eyes crinkling. "I'd like that."

"Okay, well Eric's not here, but some of the guys you played cards with that night are if you want to hang out with them." She gestured to the right where the group was engrossed in a game.

"I'll just take a seat and wait. I'm not in the mood for cards."

"Right, well, I need to check on Willow. I'll speak to you later."

"Yep." He walked away, toward the group of couches by the window. Only once he'd seated himself did she finally turn and join Willow. She didn't need to be that close to her animal, but at the moment she wanted the peace her companion provided. Her thoughts were whirling a million miles a minute.

Caleb had come to see her. What did that mean? What did he want? More to the point, did she want what he was offering?

The next hour dragged slower than molasses. Why, Kerry had no idea. Willow did her job and Kerry joked with the people around her.

As she clipped Willow's lead to her collar, she noticed Caleb in conversation with George as well as the lead trainer from the organization that handled Willow's training.

It was a surprise to see Bill here, but not unusual. He

popped in now and then, unannounced, to observe the dogs.

She wandered over there. "Hey, Bill, good to see you."

"Kerry, great to see you too." Bill reached over and gave her a quick hug before squatting down to scratch Willow behind the ears. "And a hello to you, young lady. I watched you doing your stuff. You're doing an awesome job." He crooned, and as if Willow understood every single word, her body shook with excitement.

"If I didn't know better, I'd say you just made her day," Caleb commented lightly, canting his head in Willow's direction.

Bill stood and laughed. "I'm sure they understand what I say to them. I often get weird looks from people when I talk to dogs as if they're humans. Sometimes the conversation with them is better than with people I know."

"I'm sure," he murmured.

Kerry watched the byplay between the two men. For having just met, they seemed to have fallen into a comfortable space.

"Well, the only reason she's good at her job, Bill, is because of you and your training," Kerry said.

"Thanks, Kerry, but really dogs like Willow make it look easy. I've had my fair share of dog owners who are convinced their dog will make a good therapy dog. Unfortunately, not all are suitable."

"Same with K-9 dogs," Caleb interjected. "It's all about temperament and trainability. I've seen dogs from the same litter have completely different results. One dog was attentive and took to the training regime like a duck to water. And another dog got distracted by the simplest things."

Kerry had to stop her jaw from dropping open. Caleb volunteered information about his background to someone he'd just met, without any prompting. That had to be a good thing, though she didn't miss the flash of pain in his eyes as he spoke. If she didn't know better, she'd say he was waging an inner war with himself. But what was causing the struggle?

Bill nodded. "I've spoken to people who train dogs for the blind, and they say the same thing. A dog can go through all the aspects of training, only to be tripped up at the very end by something as simple as barking at everyone who walks past."

Bill glanced at his watch and grimaced. "Oops, I'm going to be late for a meeting if I don't get out of here. Great to see you again, Kerry, Willow."

She gave Bill another hug. "You too, Bill. I'll call about getting over to the facility to do a little more training with Willow."

"Sounds good." The other man nodded and then turned to Caleb, again holding his hand out. "Caleb, great to meet and chat with you. Call me if you need anything in the future."

"Will do." Caleb shook Bill's hand.

"Well, then I guess I should be going too," George

commented, startling Kerry. He'd not said a word, but that was George, always observing, and when he thought it necessary, he'd speak his mind. "Caleb, good to see you again. Don't be a stranger here. We can always do with help. Have a good day, you two... well, three." He finished on a chuckle as he patted Willow on the head.

Wait, was Caleb looking at leaving the air force? It almost sounded like he'd been given two job opportunities. Although he did mention being on medical leave.

There were so many questions she wanted to ask Caleb, but she wasn't in a place where she could.

"Do you want to take that walk now?" he asked, his hand sliding to the small of her back. A shiver of heat coursed through her, firing her senses to life.

Willow barked as though Caleb's question had been directed to her. Kerry laughed. "I guess Willow is a smart cookie and wants to go for a walk."

Caleb's fingers trailed up her spine, and she bit her lip to prevent a moan of pleasure from escaping. "I guess so, but how about Willow's owner?"

His voice had dropped a couple of octaves, and Kerry had visions of that tone in her ear seconds before he thrust into her body.

"Yes, a walk. Let's walk." She took off out of the room, not sure who she was trying to escape, Caleb or her visions of them in bed. Visions she wanted to make come true.

What on earth was she thinking?

Chapter Thirteen

THE SUN BEAT down on Caleb's head as he followed Kerry's retreating figure out the door and into the grassy area at the back of the building. Memories of another time he and Kerry were in this area slammed into him. His fingers were still tingling from the brief contact with her back. He'd love to know what had made her jumpy though. One second she'd been melting into his touch and the next she'd moved away from him as though she'd been electrocuted.

Willow kept glancing over her shoulder to ensure he still followed them. It wouldn't take much to increase his stride length and keep time with Kerry. But there was a reason she wanted the space between them, and he would give it to her. Hopefully, it didn't mean she was trying to work out a way to stop anything developing between them before it even started.

She went to the bench where they'd sat the night they'd shared their first kiss.

Did she replay it over in his mind like he did?

He joined her on the warm wood, making sure to keep a

respectable distance between them, even though he wanted nothing more than to sling an arm around her shoulder and bring her close.

Her fingers twisted Willow's pink sparkly lead, a sure sign of nerves. Willow sat on the grass, looking up at the two humans, her tongue lolling out of her mouth as she panted.

"Damn, I should've brought some water for her," Kerry muttered beside him.

"We can go back in if you'd like." Not ideal, but he'd do anything for that little dog. Leaning forward, he scooped her up and placed her on his lap. The dog let out a sigh of contentment.

Kerry shook her head and smiled. "I don't think she'd be happy if I moved her now."

His fingers tangled in the short course hair. "No, I don't think so either."

Silence stretched between them and Caleb couldn't form the words he needed. But if they had any hope of exploring this attraction growing between them, everything had to be laid on the line.

Taking a deep breath, he willed his mind to form words that made sense. "I'm currently on medical leave. I have a meeting with my commanding officer in the next couple of days to hear the medical board's finding. I'll know if I will stay in the air force or be medically discharged with full benefits."

Saying the words out loud made them real, and he waited for the pain that pierced his chest, like it always did when he thought about his future.

It didn't come.

Had his subconscious been working quietly in the background preparing him for this moment?

A warm hand laid over his on Willow's back. Kerry's breast brushed up against his arm, and his body responded immediately. *Settle down. Now is not the time or the place.* But the future, definitely.

"I'm sorry. That must be a hard decision to have to make."

"It's not easy, but one I have to anyway."

"What are your options?" she asked, her fingers stroking the top of his palm gently.

Willow lifted her head and laid it over Kerry's leg. From the dog's perspective, her two favorite people were close and all was right in her world.

"I could take a desk job in the security forces division. Perhaps go into a high school or college and work with their ROTC program, which I can do even if I get discharged. Or I could find something else to do entirely. I'm not far off my twenty years so I would've had to think about my future anyway."

When he'd joined the military, he'd never imagined he'd reach twenty years' service. After surviving basic training, his goal had been to finish his enlistment time and then leave. Yet he'd grown to love what he did and he loved working with the dogs, so he'd kept reenlisting.

His father had been so proud of him. In a way, he was glad Dad wasn't here to see him struggle with this decision. Although knowing Martin Bradshaw, he would've told his son there was no shame in retiring after twenty years.

"Sounds like you don't like any of those options."

"I know that working behind a desk isn't for me. And while an ROTC program could be good, I don't think it's for me either."

"So if they don't discharge you, when your twenty years are up you'll retire and find something else to do?"

Caleb closed his eyes and focused inwardly. Willow's rhythmic panting soothing him. He opened his eyes and faced Kerry. "I think that's what I'm going to do."

"You don't sound so sure. Changing your whole life is a big decision to make. *Thinking* that's what you want to do isn't the way to go. You have to *want* it. You have to know"—she placed her hand over his heart—"deep in here, that what you're doing is what's best for you. Your mind will convince you what you should do. But your heart will let you know if it's the right decision."

Every word was true. He'd arrived at the center today convinced being medically discharged wasn't all that bad. Yet seeing the guys playing their cards, some laughing, some lost in their thoughts and pain, doubts had crept in. He joined the military to protect and serve his country. He could still do that behind a desk. Even inspire young people to join the air force through the ROTC program.

But would it make him happy?

He didn't know.

It didn't help that both George and Bill had spoken to him about how important former veterans were to their organizations.

"I still have a lot to think about. I was sure I'd made up my mind earlier today. Now, I don't know."

"Don't feel bad about wavering from one decision to another. I'm guessing if you hadn't had your accident, you wouldn't be in this position."

Accident.

He referred to what happened to him as an accident, but it wasn't really. They'd been ambushed when they'd least expected it.

"Yeah, if it hadn't had happened, I'd probably be overseas now, or at least I'd been going to and from base every day to work out and train with my squadron. Instead I sit at home and do nothing."

Her hand clasped his again and he placed his other one over the top, anchoring her to him.

"I'm sorry, Caleb. I don't claim to understand what it is you're going through, but I've been at a crossroads when I'd least expected it. I can't deny it's daunting not knowing what you're going to do from day to day, but then you find it and waking up isn't so difficult."

"You make it sound so easy. I've spent nearly the last

year in limbo. I lost my working partner. Trigger relied on me as much as I relied on him. Knowing that I'm never going to see him again is the hardest thing I have to deal with on a day-to-day basis."

For almost twenty years, all he'd known was being in the air force. How was he ever going to find something that fulfilled him like serving his country had?

THE PAIN IN Caleb's tone was almost too much for her to bear. She wanted to comfort him. Let him know he wasn't alone. But she suspected showing him pity was the last thing he wanted.

Everything began to make sense to her. The way he'd wanted to avoid Willow when they first met. The way he constantly pushed the dog away when she tried to give him comfort. Little things that added up to form a coherent picture.

Over time, he had softened toward Willow. Yet he still held back. Even now, his hand might be resting on Willow in his lap, but it could've been a lump of wood.

"What happened to you and Trigger?" she asked and braced herself for the brush-off she was sure to be tossed at her.

Caleb tensed beside her, and it was only because their bodies were aligned side by side that she was aware of it. "We were asked to help out with an issue at the Texas/Mexico border. Trigger and I were scouring the area, looking for any individuals who may have been hiding in the scrub. We stumbled across signs of a camp. It looked like whoever was there hadn't been gone long. The next thing I knew, a group of men came over a small rise and ambushed all of us, spraying bullets everywhere. Trigger jumped up and pushed me to the ground, taking shots to the neck and chest. One whimper of pain and then he was gone. I also got shot in the shoulder and leg. We ended up getting the guys and found out they were part of one of the large Mexican drug cartels. They're now awaiting trial and will, in all likelihood, be extradited to Mexico once convicted. Although I'm not sure. I know I'll have to testify at some stage."

Every word that came out of his mouth was so clinical and emotionless. Her heart broke for him. Like anything, one moment in time changed a person's destiny in a way they never, ever expected or wanted.

Kerry laid her head on his shoulder, unable to stop the tears from falling. "I know they're hollow words, but I'm so sorry. So sorry this happened to you and Trigger."

The hand he'd had resting on Willow cupped her head, keeping her close to him. A tiny bit of tension eked out of her. At least he wasn't pushing her away. "Thank you. I know I should talk about him more. But it's hard."

Willow shifted her position and snuggled into the both of them, offering her silent support. "I have no doubt.

Talking helps though."

Caleb sighed and his fingers drifted from the back of her head to her shoulder. "It's not easy to rehash defining moments in your past. It unlocks the 'what if' parts of your mind. What if I'd seen the flash of gun earlier? Perhaps I could've ducked and Trigger would still be with me. What if I'd gone in a different direction?"

"Stop," she said softly. "That's not helping. Going over it all doesn't make it any better. It only makes it hurt more. You can't change what happened in the past."

Caleb moved quickly, before she even had a chance to register it. He scooped Willow off his lap and put her on the ground. Then he was up, pacing back and forth in front of her. "You think I don't know that? I *know* I can't change what happened. I can't bring back Trigger. I can't bring back the guys who died. I have to live with this every single day." He thrust an arm toward the building. "Every single guy in there has moments like this. Each and every one wishes they could've done something different and have to live with the fact that they can't. Have to live with the fact that they're alive and their friends aren't."

Kerry stood and hooked the looped handle of Willow's lead over one of the wooden slats of the bench. There were professionals not fifty feet away who could help him through this, but she had an idea he wouldn't want anyone to see him like this.

With careful steps, she made her way to where he now

stood, hands in pocket, gazing out over the lake. What she was about to do was a huge gamble, but one she would take and deal with the consequences afterward.

She slipped her arms around his waist and hugged him tight. She opened her mouth and then closed it again.

What could she say that would take away his pain?

Nothing.

Nothing would take it away except time and perhaps the advice from a professional. But she could provide him with support and comfort. Let him know he was not alone.

His hand closed over hers and a long sigh rippled out of him. She imagined he blew out a lot of pain with that breath.

"I'm so lost. Some days I think I've got my shit together and then others it's clear I haven't. I had a clear vision in my mind when I came here today. The second I walked into the room and saw you and Willow working, everything blurred, and now I'm adrift without any idea of what to do next."

Caleb was sharing a part of him with her that he probably hadn't shared with anyone.

"I'm here. Whenever you need to talk or whatever, I'm here."

He turned in her arms and loosely gripped her hips. "I know. As I said, it's hard to talk about things."

She reached up and smoothed his furrowed brow. "There are lots of people who will listen, apart from me. Some are right in that building over there. All you have to do is take a leap of faith."

Oh boy, what had she just said? She'd committed to being there for him. But she'd never gone back on her word before, and she wasn't about to start now, no matter how scared she was that she couldn't help him when he needed it.

Chapter Fourteen

AFTER A LONG, emotional day with Caleb, she'd been hoping for a nice, calm evening at the restaurant. Of course, fate had other ideas and she'd had to deal with her temperamental head chef, a new hostess who cried at the drop of a hat, and a couple of impatient diners who hadn't wanted to wait five minutes while they cleared a table for them. It had taken some fast talking, but she'd smoothed everyone's ruffled feathers.

Unfortunately, collapsing on her bed and sleeping for twelve hours was a luxury she didn't have. Dreaming about it was allowed though.

As she walked into her kitchen, she noticed the living room light was still on. Why was Dad still up? Had something happened to him? Had he fallen and not been able to get up? If he had fallen, perhaps he'd knocked himself out.

Stop it.

Willow scampered down the hallway to meet Kerry. If there were anything wrong, her dog would be letting her know.

"Hey, girl," she said as she bent down and picked her up,

cuddling into her warm body. "Did you have a good night?"

Willow nuzzled her neck as she pushed her little legs against Kerry's belly in an attempt to get higher on her shoulder.

"I don't think you'll get much higher. I'm not that tall." She chuckled as she walked to the living room. She found her father asleep in front of the television, the sound low. She popped Willow down, turned the TV off, and wandered over to where Dad lay asleep.

"Hey, sleepyhead, come on! Time to wake up and go to bed."

"Loretta?" her dad mumbled, and he blinked a couple of times. "Oh, hey, sweetie, it's you. Sorry. I guess I feel asleep."

Her heart skipped a beat. The chances of Mom waking him up in the last couple of years of her life would've been pretty slim. Her ability to move independently had been taken from her three years prior to her death.

"Yeah, you did. How come you didn't go to bed earlier?"

Dad struggled to sit up a little straighter and reached over to the pile of papers on the side table. "I wanted to wait until you came home. There was something in the mail for you I wanted to talk to you about."

Since when did her dad look through her mail? She was an adult. She made her own decisions. Sometimes they weren't the best decisions, Winthorn being one. But ever since she'd gotten herself away from him, she'd finished college. Purchased a house. Found a dream job.

Caleb.

Well, she didn't know if she had Caleb, but there was definitely a connection between them. One they'd each acknowledged feeling.

She held her hand out for the letter. "Can I have it please?"

Her father handed over the envelope. It was still sealed; at least he hadn't opened it. But why did he want to talk to her about it then?

Kerry looked at the return address. "Huh? Lawton and Lawton. They weren't Mom's lawyers, were they?"

"No. That's what concerns me. Why do you have lawyers contacting you? Are you up to date with your student loan and mortgage payment?"

Kerry resisted the urge to roll her eyes. She was thirty years old. If Dad hadn't broken his legs, he wouldn't know anything about the letter. "Yes, Dad, I'm up to date. My student loan is pretty much paid off. Because I only had one semester to go, I only had to take out a small loan to cover the cost of the course and books. The mortgage is automatically deducted from my bank account, along with all my other bills."

She ripped the envelope open and pulled out the piece of stiff yellow paper. Unfolding it, she tried to make sense of the legalese printed on the sheet.

After the third read, her blood began to boil. "The sneaky, low life bastard. How could he do this to me?"

"Who and do what?" Dad asked as he stood beside her on his crutches.

"Winthorn Hartigan the third, that's who. He's demanding I repay him the money he spent on me while I lived with him. The conservative amount is thirty thousand dollars. The letter says Winthorn believes it's more but is willing to be generous and not ask for the full amount. Oh my God, what a jerk. Can he do this to me? Can he make me pay him back for when I was living with him?"

Her dad wrapped his arm around her shoulder, leaning on her, and she stumbled a fraction before gaining her balance. Nothing good would come of it if they both tumbled to the ground. "I'm not sure, Kerry. I don't think so. It's not like you were married or anything."

"But we lived together for more than seven years, Dad. Would that make it a common law marriage?"

"I think we need to speak to a lawyer."

She sighed, tiredness seeping into every pore of her body.

This isn't over, Kerry. Mark my words. You'll regret not taking the time to talk to me tonight.

Seemed Winthorn made good on his threat. She did regret not talking to him that night. But would it have made any difference? Clearly, he wanted money from her. Money she didn't have.

"What am I going to do?" she whispered. If she did have to pay him back, she'd have to sell her house. Or she supposed she could check into how much equity she had in the place. The inheritance she received from Mom had been a substantial amount, meaning she only had a small mortgage. But the last thing she wanted to do was refinance. She could probably afford a higher mortgage payment, but it was one she didn't want.

"Kerry, sweetie, it'll be fine. We'll work through this together. I'm not going to let that bastard do anything more to hurt you again. I may have let you down by not seeing what was right in front of me, but not this time."

"Thank you, Dad. I love you."

"I love you too, sweetie," he responded and kissed her on the forehead. "Now I think the best thing would be for us to get some sleep, and in the morning we can read through it again and plot a course of action."

"Sounds good to me."

Once she was happy that Dad would be able to get into bed without any issues, she gave him another hug and headed to her room, pausing in the doorway. "You know what, Dad?"

"What sweetie?"

"I know it sounds terrible, but I'm kind of glad you hurt yourself and had to come stay with me. I like having you around."

"Me too. And I like being around you too."

"Night, Dad."

"Night, Kerry. Sleep well."

KERRY STAGGERED INTO the kitchen the next morning, wishing she loved the taste of coffee, because a shot of caffeine would be what she needed right now. Sleep had been elusive, as she'd suspected it would be after reading the lawyer's letter.

Willow had wandered out a few minutes ago, and the second her four little legs carried her in through the doggie door, Willow would be demanding breakfast.

Opening the fridge, Kerry grabbed out the can of food and scooped a portion into the ceramic bowl and set it on the floor where Willow would find it when she came back in.

Kerry flopped into a kitchen chair and laid her head on the table over her crossed arms, her eyes drifting shut, but she kept her ears open for the telltale clipping of her dog's nails on the tiled floor.

Today was her day off, and her initial plan had been to make use of the massage voucher Dad had given her when she'd gotten her job. But now that plan was out the window. Calling lawyers and hopefully meeting with one to determine that Winthorn didn't have a leg to stand on was on the schedule now.

Why the hell was he coming after her for money? It wasn't like she asked him to pay for everything. He wouldn't let her work. Wouldn't let her out of the house to try to make a contribution to their funds.

Whenever she'd approached the subject after she'd dropped out of her final semester of college, he'd told her she was his princess and he wanted to look after her. Give her everything she wanted. In the end, she gave up trying to get a job, but one thing she did do was make sure she didn't spend hours shopping at the most expensive stores in Dallas.

The request for the reimbursement of thirty thousand dollars she'd supposedly frittered away made no sense.

Dammit, she wanted her mind to stop buzzing with questions. Questions she was well aware the answers to might not be what she wanted.

She yawned and glanced at the clock, sitting up straighter. Twenty minutes had passed since she'd walked into the kitchen. Over twenty minutes since Willow went outside.

"Damn dog. She hasn't gone over to Caleb's, has she? He said he'd fix the gap she got through," she muttered as she strode back to her room to put on something other than her pajamas to go searching for her dog.

"What's up, sweetie?" Dad called out.

Pausing, she took two steps back and poked her head around his door. He'd propped himself up on one elbow and looked like he was about to attempt to get out of bed.

"Nothing."

"Didn't sound like nothing."

She sighed. He'd only badger her if she didn't spill. "Fine. It looks like Willow's escaped again. I don't know what it is about her need to go hassle Caleb."

Dad chuckled and settled himself back down again. "She loves him, and as much as he doesn't want to admit it, she soothes him."

"Well, I wish she wouldn't disappear on me though. What if it weren't Caleb living next door? What if it were a horrid person who complained when she barked and threatened to do something about shutting her up permanently?"

"You don't have to worry about Caleb doing anything like what you've suggested. He may have tried to push Willow away when he first started looking after me, but she won him over. There's no way he'd hurt her. Plus, if it weren't Caleb living next door, she wouldn't escape."

"I hope you're right, but I'm sure he doesn't want to be constantly bothered by her little out-of-the-blue house calls. I'll be back in a few, then I can get started on breakfast for you. We've got a busy day ahead of us."

"Invite Caleb over for breakfast. It's the least you can do," he called as she disappeared into her room.

Yeah right, like Caleb would want to come over for breakfast after baring his soul to her. Conversation had been sparse on their walk back to the center.

She grabbed a pair of shorts from her drawer and shoved her legs in. All through her shift, she'd been tempted to send him a text to see how he was doing. She'd held back because she didn't want to make him feel uncomfortable for sharing his secret with her.

She slipped her feet into her flip-flops and grabbed one

of the leads she had in her room. Grabbing her keys off the hallway table, she flicked the lock and pulled the door open.

"Ooph," she mumbled as she walked into a wall of course dog hair and a sense of déjà vu swept over her like a warm cocoon. Stepping back, she looked up and smiled. "I feel like we've done this before."

Unlike last time when Caleb all but shoved Willow into her arms, he shifted the dog higher on his chest and laughed. "Yeah, I'm getting the same sensation."

Willow had the biggest doggie smile on her face, as if to say, *Look, Mommy. I brought you a treat.*

A treat indeed. Caleb hadn't bothered to put a shirt on, so his shoulders glowed golden in the early morning sunshine peeping through the trees.

"I'm so sorry about her bothering you again," she said as she waved Caleb inside. "I thought you said you were going to fix the place where she came through."

If she hadn't been watching him, she wouldn't have seen the slight flush rising up his neck and blooming across his cheeks. "I, uh, haven't got round to fixing it yet."

Interesting. If she didn't know better, she'd almost think he hadn't repaired it on purpose. But then that would mean he wanted Willow to continue to visit him, and she couldn't quite believe that to be true.

"Can I tempt you into staying for breakfast as a way of thanking you for not being annoyed with her surprise visits?"

Caleb put Willow on the ground and she scampered off

down the hall. He stood a hairsbreadth away from her. Her line of vision was filled with a well-defined, slightly hairy bare chest. Without conscious thought, she placed her hands against his pectoral muscles, the skin warm beneath her fingers. No wonder Willow was smiling happily. Who wouldn't want to be snuggling up to this chest?

His fingers closed over hers and she wondered, for half a heartbeat, if he was going to push her hands away. Instead, he squeezed them, forcing her gaze up to meet his.

Heat flared in their dark depths. "Morning, Kerry," he murmured before lowering his head and capturing her lips.

The last thing she predicted would happen when she opened the door and ran into him would be that a few minutes later she'd be wrapped up in his arms and they'd be sharing a warm kiss on her doorstep. She definitely could get used to it.

It registered that the door was still open and they were giving quite the show to anyone who walked past. Managing to squeeze her hand out from between them, she reached out until she connected with the lump of wood. She gave it a push, and the door slammed shut with a resounding *thud*.

She was aware of Willow barking in the background, but her focus was totally on the man in her arms. The way his mouth moved over hers. He, too, had shifted and his arms now banded around her, bringing her flush against him. His desire for her evident in the hard ridge of his erection against her belly.

Maybe Willow was playing matchmaker with her and Caleb. Willow was the only reason she'd run into Caleb all those weeks ago. Perhaps Dad had been right, if Caleb didn't live next door, her dog would stay in her backyard.

A throat clearing finally penetrated the hazy fog his kiss had cast over her. A fog she didn't want to dissipate. She wanted to hug it close; she'd never experienced the wave of emotions tumbling through her when she'd been kissed by anyone else, even Winthorn, and for a time she'd thought he was the one and only for her.

Caleb slowly withdrew his lips, but he didn't relinquish his hold. If anything, he tightened his grip. "Morning, Ron. How are you this morning?"

Mortification replaced her desire. How could she have forgotten her dad was a few feet away? Even as a teenager, she'd never been busted kissing someone. It had to happen when she was thirty, a homeowner, and held down a responsible job. And not once but twice Dad had caught them kissing in the hallway.

"I see Kerry found you and Willow." She didn't need to turn around to see if Dad was smiling. She heard it in his tone.

"You could say that."

"I take it you're joining us for breakfast?" her dad asked, as if she weren't standing in Caleb's arms not three feet away from him.

Determined to get herself back in charge of things, she

wiggled out of Caleb's arms. He turned his back quickly so her dad couldn't see the front of his sweats, as the light flannel did nothing to hide his arousal. If she weren't so embarrassed herself, she'd laugh at the situation.

Straightening her shoulders, she looked her dad in the eye. His eyes twinkled, and he winked at her.

"I'm just going to the kitchen."

"Sounds good, sweetie. We'll be there in a few minutes. I think Caleb needs a little time to, uh, compose himself."

"Oh. My. God. Dad, you did not just say that!" Her cheeks burned brighter than the burner flame in the kitchen at the restaurant. As she stomped past him, he laughed loudly at his own joke. Caleb joined in, and she mentally threw her hands up in the air.

Men.

Last night, she said she liked having Dad live with her. Now she wasn't so sure. There was a reason adults lived by themselves and not with their parents—no unwanted interruptions. Although interrupting her and Caleb probably wasn't a bad thing. His kisses shocked the hell out of her, especially after how tense things between them had been last night.

She pulled out the carton of eggs and package of bacon from the fridge. Give her a smoothie or an apple any day. But Dad liked to have a cooked breakfast, so she broke some eggs into a bowl, added milk, and began to whip them together, her gaze falling on the letter sitting in the middle of the table. She should move it. For a few minutes, her mind had shed the worries and she savored being held by Caleb.

As if drawn by an invisible force, she walked over to the table and looked again at the letter. The black typeface blurred together.

"Can I help with anything?"

The bowl slipped, but she caught it before it could crash to the ground. "Jesus, Caleb, don't scare me like that."

Her heart pounded a million miles an hour. "Sorry. I thought you heard me come in."

Tucking the bowl tighter against her body, she reached for the letter on the table. The last thing she wanted was for him to see what trouble was knocking on her doorstep. Unfortunately, he was quicker.

Her breath whooshed out when it looked like he was going to hand it to her, but then he pulled the paper out of her reach.

Damn.

CALEB READ THE words for a second and then looked up at Kerry. A stricken expression highlighted her features along with the faint pink hue of embarrassment.

"What's all this about?" he asked. He didn't have any place inquiring about the contents. A letter he shouldn't have picked up in the first place. He was well acquainted with keeping his life private, but this was Kerry. The woman he was beginning to care for. He couldn't deny he'd been delighted to see Willow sitting on his back porch when he opened the door to her bark.

Now he couldn't help but wonder if the dog didn't have an ulterior motive for her unannounced visit to his place. Somehow, some way, Willow had known her owner was troubled and had come looking for him.

Well, it worked, and here he stood in the kitchen with a letter from a law firm stating Kerry owed a man by the name of Winthorn Hartigan the third a large amount of money.

With a pretentious name like that, he had to be an asshole.

"Nothing that concerns you." She held out her hand. "Can I have my letter back, please?"

Yeah, he'd clearly overstepped his mark. He handed over the paper. She slammed it face down on the table and walked over to the cooktop, placing the bowl down on the counter with a loud bang.

He might not have been in any serious relationships in his life, but he'd heard enough stories from the guys about dealing with angry wives or partners. The difference between their situations and his was that he and Kerry hadn't really argued. She was already upset when he walked into the kitchen.

If he continued on in the vein he'd planned when he walked into the kitchen, she might relax around him and tell him the story behind the letter. "Where's your toaster? I can get started on some toast while you cook the eggs."

"It's fine. You don't have to help. You're a guest." Her words so polite, as if she were addressing a stranger and not a man who she'd kissed back with a passion he'd never encountered before just moments ago.

His dick twitched against the soft fabric of his sweats. He'd only just gotten his aroused body under control. A mundane task like making toast would help to keep his mind off him and Kerry and a bed that was only a few feet away. "Please, I want to help. And I'm sorry for taking the letter off you. I had no right."

"You're right. You shouldn't have. That was my private mail. I don't think you'd like if I did it to you."

"No, I wouldn't. I don't know what came over me."

"Let me say one thing. My life is my own. I make my own decisions and deal with my own problems. No one else. Do you understand?"

Fire lit her eyes, and he admired that strength. He'd been an asshole, snatching her letter. He was lucky she wasn't going to kick him out. "Everything you've said is true. I'm really sorry for what I did, Kerry."

She blew out a frustrated breath and he'd won the battle. "Fine. Toaster is in the lower cabinet by the oven."

They worked together in harmony, and he resisted the urge to pull her into his arms again and kiss her. After the letter fiasco, that would be the last thing he should do.

Willow had wandered into the kitchen and lay on the ground, her head resting on her paws, as if she approved of the sight in front of her.

For the first time since his accident and the uncertainty of his career, Caleb had a sense of what his life could be if he only took the plunge. It was no hardship picturing mornings where he and Kerry made breakfast together. Maybe even fed each other in bed, followed by a session of explosive love-making.

Explosive lovemaking?

Sheesh, what was he, a hero in a romance novel?

All he and Kerry had shared were a couple of hot kisses. Although he couldn't deny it—he wouldn't mind taking it further. As cheesy as the thought was, he had no doubt that when he and Kerry finally did make love it would be explosive.

Yeah, he could be a hero in a romance novel.

"Caleb? Are you okay?"

"Sorry, yeah. I was just… uh… thinking."

"Thinking? That's all?"

"Yeah, why?"

She slammed the spatula she was holding down on the counter. "Because I thought you were in the middle of some sort of PTSD attack. I was talking to you, but you were looking at me with a blank stare."

He smoothed his hands over her shoulders and pulled her in for a hug. "I'm sorry, honey. I didn't mean to scare you. I'm fine." He pulled back so he could look into her eyes. "I'm more than fine."

Giving in to the temptation he'd been trying to fight since he walked into the kitchen, he lowered his head as she raised hers. Their lips met in a soft kiss. He enjoyed holding her and being part of what he hoped they would become—a couple.

A nudge against his leg made him pull away from Kerry, his hands resting lightly on her hips. "Willow, you're going to have to learn some boundaries."

The dog barked and wagged her tail enthusiastically. Kerry turned her attention back to the eggs cooking in the pan. "I don't think you can do any wrong in Willow's eyes. I think she's in love."

Caleb's heart stuttered. The *L* word. He focused back on the toast, putting a little more distance between him, Kerry, and Willow.

Admitting that he wanted to pursue Kerry didn't necessarily mean he had any plans to fall in love with her. Or her dog. His heart was still raw from the loss of Trigger and then losing his father quickly after the accident.

Guilt. A constant companion. Trigger would still be alive if he'd been more aware. His dad would still be alive if he hadn't been driving to see Caleb in the hospital.

"Okay, everything's done. How's the toast?"

He pasted a smile on his face. "All done."

Kerry cocked her head, studying him. He held her gaze,

NICOLE FLOCKTON

hoping he managed to keep his discomfort off his face. "Good. You can take it to the table."

He carried over the platter, setting it down next to the steaming plate of scrambled eggs and bacon. Out of the corner of his eye, he noticed Kerry studying the letter again before throwing it on the counter. She'd advised him it was none of his business, but he couldn't ignore the troubled look on her face even if he wanted to.

Later, he'd bring it up with her later. When they were alone and her father wasn't a witness to it. Perhaps Ron didn't even know about the guy demanding Kerry pay him back a huge amount.

What had she done? Who was Winthorn Hartigan the third to Kerry? And should he worry that this was all a ploy by Winthorn to get Kerry back?

Chapter Fifteen

THE LAWYER'S LETTER mocked Kerry as she sat at the kitchen table, alone now that Caleb had left and her dad had gone to take a shower. The urge to burn the offending piece of paper was strong.

Sighing, she pushed back from the table and picked up the document, scanning the words she'd read thirty times over already.

"What are you going to do about it, sweetie?"

Kerry's head whipped up at the sound of her father's voice. She had been lost in her own thoughts that she hadn't paid attention to the shower stopping and her dad entering the kitchen, fully dressed. "Fight Winthorn, but to do that I'm going to have to employ the services of one of the top solicitors in San Antonio, and that's an expense I'm not sure I can manage."

Her dad's large, warm hand closed over her clenched fist. "I know, and I'll help you. It's not right what this jerk is doing to you. Not happening on my watch."

No way would she let her father use his hard-earned retirement funds on her. She'd make it work, and if, at the end of the day, she'd have to sell the house to pay him back, then she would. "I won't have you doing that, Dad. This is my problem and I'll handle it."

He pulled his hand away and crossed his arms over his chest. "Oh, me helping you isn't up for discussion. It's how it's going to be. You're my daughter and I'm going to fight alongside you. And I will help you financially in any way I can."

Kerry stared at Dad, surprised at the vehemence in his voice. What could she say? When she'd informed her parents she wasn't finishing college, even though she only had one semester to go, Dad had told her she'd regret her decision. At the time she'd been convinced Winthorn hung the moon. If only she'd listened to her father's concerns then, she wouldn't be in this position now.

You also wouldn't have Willow and you wouldn't have met Caleb.

Well, one of those things still would've happened. She would've gotten a dog, but maybe not Willow… okay, if she hadn't gone through what she had, her life wouldn't be what it was today. Accepting her dad's help didn't mean she was weak and unable to take care of herself.

"Thank you, Dad. It means so much to me."

"Sweetie, I'll always be on your side."

"Do you think Mom's lawyers will be able to help us in this situation? And if so, seeing as we're a returning client, maybe we'll get a discounted hourly rate."

Dad laughed. "Somehow I don't think so, but they do deal with family law. Let me call them and see if I can make an appointment."

She leaned up and kissed her dad on the cheek. "Thanks. I'm going to have a shower. This isn't how I wanted to spend my day off, but if I can get this sorted out now, I'll be happy."

"Leave it with me." He patted her cheek and hobbled out of the kitchen back to his room.

Kerry folded the offending piece of paper and stuffed it in her purse. Winthorn's actions could be understandable if they'd been married, but he hadn't even discussed marriage. Oh, she'd thought about it a few times but never had the courage to mention it to him. Considering how much he controlled her life, why did he need a piece of paper to tie her to him? She was more than a willing participant in whatever he wanted.

Which made him dumping her all that more baffling. Even now, she couldn't get her head around his actions. It didn't matter because now it turned out to be the best thing he'd ever done. She'd found her feet and was living her life how she wanted.

Maybe that was it.

Maybe he'd seen how she hadn't fallen apart and collapsed into a piece of worthless trash after their breakup and he didn't like it. Perhaps he'd been hoping she'd come groveling back to him, begging for him to reconsider his decision.

It had to be a thorn in his side that she'd picked herself up, dusted herself off, and tackled life full steam ahead. And she'd been successful too.

This scenario made perfect sense. Well, she hadn't shattered when he'd dumped her and she wasn't going to shatter now with his threats. If he wanted a fight, he was going to get one.

And she was going to win.

CALEB CHECKED HIS clothes to make sure there were no creases that shouldn't be there. His shoes shined brighter than a brand-new penny, and his hair was slicked back so as not to show how much he really needed to get a haircut.

Wearing his uniform again after being out of it for so long felt foreign in a way it never had before. It was almost like he was playing dress up and the clothes didn't fit right.

He raised his fist and knocked on Lieutenant Commander Blue's door.

"Enter."

How was it possible for the word to appear to boom around the hallway through a wooden door?

Taking a deep breath, he opened the door. The desk was immaculate, like Blue's uniform. He waved Caleb in while he scribbled on the lone piece of paper centered precisely in front of him.

Closing the door, Caleb crossed the small office and waited until his superior officer looked up, saluting the man when he did.

"Take a seat, Bradshaw."

"Thank you, sir."

Caleb sat, back rigid, as if he were undergoing a uniform inspection prior to a parade.

"You're looking well," the other man said eventually.

He relaxed his shoulders a fraction. "Thank you, sir. I'm feeling well."

"I'm glad you're here. This isn't how things are usually done. Normally, a military personnel flight contacts you, but I wanted to be the one to pass on the board's finding."

Caleb's heart beat out a rapid tattoo. He'd gone in for his final testing the day before and after he completed them, even he was aware his ability to perform his job had decreased.

"Thank you, sir." What else could he say? Regardless of the fact he'd been preparing for this, now that the moment was on him, he wasn't sure he wanted to hear the outcome.

His life was about to change, like the day he signed the papers to enlist. Then, he'd been a boy full of wonder and hope. Excited about the new adventures he was about to embark on. And naïve in the sense he had no idea what basic training was going to be like. Naïve in that what he'd seen in the movies when soldiers went into battle was a combination of reality and Hollywood. Nothing could prepare him for the shouts of everyone around him and the noise from the bullets and explosions. Now he could be facing the end of his dream career.

Blue reached for a folder and opened it. "Based on the results from the tests, the doctors have determined that while you would be unable to perform your job in the way that you previously did, your experience and skills can be used in a training role with new recruits to the K-9 program."

Caleb leaned back in his chair. He hadn't anticipated this news at all. He fully expected to hear that he was about to be discharged. Did he want to be a trainer? It would mean he'd be around dogs on a daily basis. Could he do it? Could he watch the relationships between dog and handler being built, knowing it could change in a flash?

"What are you thinking, Bradshaw?" Blue interrupted his thoughts.

"To be honest, sir, I've got a lot of thoughts going through my mind. This wasn't the outcome I was expecting."

Blue shuffled through some of the papers in the folder. "There is another option for you."

Caleb knew exactly what he was talking about. Retirement. He'd come to the meeting prepared to end his career in the air force. Had accepted it and, yeah, that was what he wanted. The time had come to move on. His life had changed over the last few weeks and he liked the direction it was heading. Visiting the veterans' center had been an eye-opener too.

A weight lifted off his shoulders; his decision was the right one for him. "Yes, sir. I know what you're talking about and I appreciate the medical board's finding, but I'm coming up to twenty years in service and I've decided to retire. I think this is what's best for me going forward."

Blue sat back in his chair, the hinges squeaking a little at the motion. Caleb imagined the next time he came in, the chair would be quiet. He withstood Blue's scrutiny, knowing his superior officer was studying him to check that his decision wasn't hastily made.

"I see. And are you happy with this outcome?"

"Yes, sir. I am. The medical board may think I'm recovered enough for another position, but I still experience pain and I know my leg won't be the same as it was. Also, I don't..." A lump formed in his throat and he swallowed in an attempt to dislodge it. "I'm not sure I want to work with dogs, even in a training capacity. Losing Trigger was one of the hardest things I've had to go through. He saved my life, but I can't help but feel guilty that I'm still here and he's not."

God, could he sound any softer? He was an airman. He'd done numerous tours of duty and had seen his fair share of tragedy.

"I understand losing your partner is like losing part of yourself. I don't believe that I should try and change your mind. I can see in your eyes that your decision is final. Have you considered what you might do in the future? After twenty years in the service, I don't see you as the type of person who will be happy sitting around the house."

Caleb chuckled. "You're right, sir, that's not me."

Although it had been. Until Kerry and Willow came into his life, the only times he'd left the house had been to go to rehab and to the odd party, and that had been because Ethan had forced him. Or the girl he was sleeping with at the time dragged him out of the house.

Now, since a corgi dog turned up unannounced in his backyard, he'd begun to interact with people again. It was a good feeling.

"As for my future, I've got a couple of ideas. Nothing set in concrete. I'm going to take my time and find something that really speaks to me."

"I think that's a good idea. If you need any recommendations, let me know. I know some people in the police force if you wish to go into the K-9 unit." Caleb opened his mouth to protest, but Blue held up his hand. "I know you said you don't want to work with dogs again, but they need trainers and you'd be good at it. The medical board recognized that too."

No, training dogs for action where they could be hurt or die wasn't an occupation that he would like. Of course, there were other training opportunities with dogs he could consider. But he didn't want to share that with Blue just yet.

"Thank you. I'll consider it."

"Do that. You'd be an excellent trainer, Caleb. You've got years of combat experience and good instincts."

"If I had good instincts, I wouldn't have bullet holes in my shoulder and leg and my partner wouldn't be dead." No way could he trust his instincts now.

"I don't think your instincts played a part in what happened to you and Trigger or the other men involved in the incident. It's how the drug cartels play, and it's something we constantly battle. There wasn't anything you could've done differently that would've changed the outcome. Also, you have to remember Trigger's job was to protect. He was protecting you."

Logically, Caleb was aware his dog had acted on his instinct, but that didn't mean Caleb liked it. But one thing he knew about being in the service; arguing with a superior officer always led down the road of extra PT exercises. Not that he had to worry about that anymore.

"Yes, sir. I may not like it and it hurts like a bitch, but I'll be forever grateful that Trigger saved my life."

"Right. Well, I'll get started on your discharge papers."

Clearly, Blue had decided time for personal chitchat was over, and Caleb couldn't agree more. Laying himself open to be examined by people wasn't his favorite pastime. He stood, grimacing at the short stab of pain in his thigh. No amount of physical therapy exercise would totally take away the reminder of what he'd endured, and he wouldn't have it any other way. "Thank you, sir. I'll await your orders."

He saluted and swiveled away, military style, and walked through the door, down the hallway, and out into the fresh air. He stood for a few moments, inhaling the familiar scents of the base. The aroma of the cafeteria cooking barbeque for lunch. The sounds of guys doing drills. Any other time he'd gone on to the base he'd experienced a longing to reverse time and make him part of the things going on around him. To feed Trigger treats when he completed the training task he'd been assigned.

Today, however, a sense of calm and peace enveloped him, confirming the decision he'd made had been the correct one.

"Hey, Caleb, dude, long time no see."

He turned at the sound of the voice behind him. An unforced smile stretched across his mouth. "Ethan, good to see you."

He closed the distance to his former roommate, holding out his hand. Ethan grabbed it and pulled him into a one-arm bro-man hug. "You're looking good. Much better than when I came back from my last tour, which wasn't that long ago."

"I am doing better, thanks."

Ethan canted his head toward the building Caleb had just left. "Do I take it you'll be back here soon?"

None of his former squadron was aware of the extent of his injury or the damage done to his leg or shoulder. It wasn't information he'd been inclined to share with them. "No, I'm done. I'll be retiring when I've done my twenty, which will be in a couple months."

"Hey, that's great. Now that I have Izzy and Junior, it's something I'll be considering when I'm closing in on my twenty." Ethan laughed and scraped a hand over his face. Caleb could see the happiness radiating out of him. "I always imagined they'd be dragging me out of here. Now, well, my priorities have changed."

If anyone knew about priorities changing, it was Caleb. Of course, Ethan's reasons were far different to his own, but all it took was one moment and it was like a train switching tracks—life veered off into a direction he hadn't been expecting.

Fatherhood and marriage was definitely a good reason to reevaluate the current path.

"How is Isabella? She must be close to having the baby. The last time I saw Eric, at the veterans' center, he mentioned Isabella was nesting. I think that's the term he used."

Ethan laughed. "Yep, she's actually a week overdue. The doctor is talking about inducing her tomorrow. I'm just here to arrange some time off."

"Hey, man, that's great. I bet you're looking forward to meeting your kid."

"Yeah, I am. I'm sure Izzy is as well. She's looking uncomfortable."

Caleb never would've guessed when he arrived to talk to

Blue that he'd be standing in the middle of the base, discussing babies. But here he was, and he had to admit, he wasn't as creeped out by it as he thought he would be.

An image of Kerry, belly round with a baby, Willow by her side while she laughed at something he said, flashed across his brain. His heart skipped a couple of beats before settling back into a steady rhythm.

What the hell?

Having a family had never been part of his overall plan in life. Once he'd hit thirty-five, he figured his chance of family was over. And after Trigger and the slump he'd fallen into, falling in love, getting married, and having kids was higher in the sky than a jet plane.

"Well, hey, good luck, man," he said, pulling his head out of said sky. "I'll wait for the texts."

Ethan laughed again. "You're definitely on the list of people getting the group text." He started to walk away but stopped and faced Caleb again. "You said you've seen Eric at the veterans' center?"

Caleb had been hoping Ethan had forgotten he'd said that. Linc and Ethan had encouraged him to head down there after he'd complained about how fucked up his life had gotten when he'd been home from the hospital for a couple of months. Caleb had blocked them at every advance. "Yeah, I've… uh…" He swallowed. "I've been visiting there a bit lately."

"Huh. Well, that's great. Eric has a good time there, and

well, if it weren't for him, I wouldn't be where I am now."

Caleb recalled how Ethan had been set up on a blind date after a bet between him and Linc. "Linc's good for something these days."

"Hey, you know he's calling himself the matchmaking king now that Izzy and I are getting married. He may want to set you up."

Once again, Kerry's smiling face blazed neon bright in his mind. "Nah, I'm good. I don't need any help."

Ethan studied him for a few more seconds. "You've met someone, and I'm not talking about a someone like Amy and the others you've dated. A girl that's special."

Caleb shook his head and sent his best you're-out-of-your-mind look Ethan's way. "Not even close. I'm happy because I've made a decision about my future. And it had nothing to do with a girl."

"Okay, you keep telling yourself that. But I hope she knows what a catch you are. I'll see you around and you've got a standing invite to our place. Use it."

With a wave of his hand, his former roommate was jogging toward the parking lot. He couldn't blame him. If he had someone like Isabella waiting for him, he'd be hotfooting it back to her as well.

Duh, you do, and you've just been imaging pictures of her knocked up. Stop trying to fool yourself.

"Shut the fuck up," he muttered to his rambling subconscious. Perhaps he needed to seek help with regard to the voice he kept hearing in his head.

Maybe he should head to the veterans' center, not to see if Kerry was there but to talk to George. He'd mentioned something about a job opportunity. Now that he would be a military-free man in a couple of months, he did need to consider his future.

And if Kerry and Willow happened to be there, well, that would be a lucky coincidence. Nothing more.

Chapter Sixteen

"SO YOU THINK this guy can help me?" Kerry asked George and grabbed the business card he held out.

"Yep, Steve's a good solicitor and, being a former vet, he'll work out a reasonable fee or maybe even give you advice pro bono. He likes helping out military personnel and their families with any family legal issues, and always works within their budget."

It turned out the lawyer who'd worked on finalizing her mom's estate was on a six-month world cruise with his wife and the other lawyer in the firm was swamped and couldn't take on any new business.

Seeking out George at the veterans' center had been a pie in the sky wish and one that had been granted.

"That's great, but I'm not a veteran nor am I military family. I don't expect to get special treatment from him."

George waved away her concerns. "Nonsense. You work here and help out the guys. That makes you part of our family."

Tears she'd been battling since the second she received the news that she'd have to find a new lawyer threatened to spill over, but she blinked rapidly. No way would she cry in front of George or anyone—she left her tears for her pillow.

"Thank you for your help. I don't know what I was expecting when I came to speak to you, but this is wonderful."

George reached across the table and patted her hand briefly. "We all love you and Willow, Kerry. Any time you need help, you know you can come here."

"Well, Willow and I love you guys, too." Kerry slipped the card in her purse and pushed back her chair. "And speaking of Willow, I should probably see what she's up to."

George stood as well, a smile creasing the corners of his eyes. "I don't think you need to worry about Willow. She's got plenty of friends here."

"Don't I know it." Kerry hitched her bag over her shoulder, pausing before striding out of his office. "I'll see you around, George."

"For sure, and keep me posted. I'll call Steve anyway and let him know you'll be in touch."

"Thanks." Her step was lighter than it had been when she walked in to the building.

Her unscheduled visit to the center had been met with a raucous welcome when the guys spied Willow trotting beside her.

As she wandered into the main game room, her breath caught in her throat. The first person she laid eyes on was Caleb.

In his uniform.

She'd always laughed at women who talked about a man in uniform and how easy it was to go weak at the knees. Kerry had seen many guys in uniform on her visits to the center, but Caleb in uniform looked completely different. Which was silly, really, considering there was nothing special about the uniform he wore to make it stand out from the others.

It simply was because it was Caleb. The man who set her heart fluttering and desire streaming through her body. The man she cared for.

Before she could examine the thought further, he looked up and their eyes met. He straightened from where he'd been squatting next to one of the guys. Willow was on the man's lap, and it pleased her to see that Caleb and Willow were ignoring each other. When Willow was on the job, it wasn't a good trait to getting distracted by other people.

Her feet couldn't move and she stared as Caleb made his way toward her, his limp barely discernable today.

"Hey," she said when he stopped in front of her.

That was the only word she was capable of saying. His citrus scent, combined with the up-close-and-personal sight of him in uniform, fried her brain synapses. His hair was slicked back in a way she hadn't seen before. It still made her want to run her fingers through it.

"Hey, yourself. I didn't think you were supposed to be here today," he said quietly.

For a second, a stab of disappointment pierced her stomach. He came hoping that he wouldn't see her.

"It's a nice surprise," he finished and then leaned down and kissed her cheek.

Her eyes fluttered shut and she swayed toward him, inhaling a hint of starch from his uniform collar. "You're looking very handsome," she said and her cheeks warmed. That had been the last thing she'd meant to say, but now that it was out there, there was no point worrying about it. "Did you decide what you're going to do now? Are you going back to work?"

Great recovery, and hopefully Caleb would concentrate on the questions and not her *very handsome* comment.

"No, not going back to work, but I did meet with my superior officer to tell him that I'm going to retire."

"That must have been tough." She could see the hurt in the depths of his brown eyes. "Are you okay?"

Time stood still for a couple of heartbeats. She reached out and brushed his hand with her fingertips.

"Yeah, it wasn't easy, but I know I did the right thing for me. And…" He took a deep breath, before bestowing a smile she'd never seen before on him. The hurt disappeared from his eyes and a sparkle entered them. "Yes, I'm okay with it."

Her lips stretched into an answering smile. "I'm glad."

Caleb curled a stray piece of hair behind her ear. A shiver rippled down her spine at the light contact. "How about we go out and celebrate my impending retirement?"

"Yes." There was no doubt in her mind. This was what

she wanted to do. Even though their first date hadn't ended spectacularly, she wanted to try again. "Yes, I'll go out and celebrate with you."

He leaned forward and pressed his lips against hers, in a quick short kiss that still had the power to ignite her senses and leave her craving more. "Good. I'll be in touch with details. I've got to go now. I've got another... uh, appointment."

"Okay, sounds good."

She watched him walk away, the navy pants hugging his ass, and heat arrowed between her thighs. Tonight couldn't come soon enough for her.

KERRY CHECKED HER appearance once last time, satisfied she looked casual and sexy. All day, her body had tingled in anticipation of her date with Caleb. She was ready to explore what lay beneath Caleb's uniform.

The doorbell rang and she took a deep breath.

"Kerry, Caleb's here." Her dad's voice carried through the house.

She checked her purse for her phone and lipstick and the condom she'd popped in there.

Never let it be said that she wasn't in charge of her destiny—an unwanted pregnancy wasn't something she wanted or needed in her life right now.

She paused outside the living room, observing the scene in front of her. Dad was sitting in his chair, leg scooter by his side. Caleb was on the couch chatting with him. The image sent her heart into overdrive. Willow was perched on Caleb's leg, a blissful doggy smile on her face as he scratched her behind the ear. He looked handsome in his dark trousers and white button-down shirt. She'd made the right decision to wear her dress.

Caleb placed Willow on the ground, and walked over to her, cupping her cheek. "Hi."

"Hey, yourself. You ready?"

"Yep, let's go."

"You two have a nice night," Dad commented from his chair.

"Thanks, Dad, and if you need anything at all, call me."

He waved away her concern. "I may still have one leg in plaster and be using a scooter, but I'm not helpless. Willow and I will be fine. And if you don't want to come home tonight, I won't bat an eyelid," he said, not in a whisper.

Oh. My. God Ground, open up and swallow me now.

"Thanks, Dad," she muttered and, giving Willow one last pat on the head, she pasted a big smile on her face."

"Bye, Ron, and don't worry. I'll take good care of her," he said as he slung an arm around her shoulder.

Kerry rolled her eyes at the double entendre. But she couldn't stop the way her body melted against his hard one.

Outside, she attempted to pull away, and after a brief

squeeze of her shoulder, he slid his hand down her arm and laced their fingers together. "This okay?" he asked.

"Yeah, it's good." Damn, he was being so sweet. She'd never had a guy ask if holding her hand was okay. "So where are we headed for dinner?"

"You'll see when we get there," he responded mysteriously. As they were headed to his house, she figured they were going to collect his car, but instead he opened his front door and stepped aside.

The second she stepped into the hallway, her senses were assailed with a mix of roses and garlic. The scents shouldn't go together, but they did. Strains of music playing softly somewhere reached her ears.

"What's going on?" she asked as he closed the door.

"Well, I thought instead of going out, I'd cook dinner for you."

"You cook?" she asked, trying to recall if they'd ever had a discussion about their cooking skills. She supposed if he lived by himself for a long while he would have had to pick up the basics. No way would Winthorn ever consider walking into a kitchen and making her a meal.

Again? What the hell was she doing thinking about him? Tonight was about her and Caleb.

Tomorrow she would go see her annoying ex and put an end to his stupid debt collector act.

"I know how to cook enough."

"Huh? What?"

"Cooking. You asked me about my culinary skills."

"Well, I'm looking forward to seeing what you've created. It smells delicious."

He chuckled and the sound slithered down her spine, firing her nerve endings to life. "Let's hope it tastes as good as it smells. Otherwise, we'll be calling for pizza."

He started toward the living room, and Kerry touched her fingers to his arm. He paused, glancing over his shoulder. The action was so damn sexy when it probably shouldn't have been. Perhaps it was because of her father's words or because of her earlier preparation should something happen. Either way, this innocent move made her wish she were brave enough to take the initiative and go for what she wanted.

"If we end up having pizza, I'm fine with that. All that matters is that I'm with you."

Time stood still as they gazed at each other in his darkened hallway, the spell broken only by the buzzing in the distance.

He cleared his throat. "Umm, that's the timer. Come have a seat in the living room. I've set out some appetizers; I'll go check on dinner."

Set out on the coffee table was a round container of what she thought was hummus with cut vegetables around it. There was also some guacamole and chips placed next to the vegetable medley. And the music was definitely coming from his phone, which was plugged into a docking station on the

TV cabinet.

None of the appetizers at the best restaurants in Dallas compared to the spread laid out in front of her.

"There's wine, but I can get you a soda or water if you want." A hint of uncertainty laced his tone, reminding her of when Caleb had told her about how he fought to not let alcohol rule his life, and her heart tumbled further into the falling-for-Caleb bucket.

"It looks great and wine sounds great." She reached to pick up one of the glasses, also resting on the table, and her hand connected with Caleb's. Electricity sparked between them, and when their eyes connected, Kerry had no doubt the desire simmering in the depths of Caleb's brown ones shimmered in her own. If her nerve endings were visible, they'd be jumping around like Mexican jumping beans. "I can get it," she said quietly. "You were about to check on dinner."

As if her words pulled him out of a fog, he smiled. "Yeah, I really don't want pizza again tonight."

She laughed, and it alleviated the sensual haze surrounding them. "I knew you didn't cook often."

Before he departed, he brushed his lips across her cheek, and her eyelids fluttered shut at the brief touch.

"I'll be back soon, so don't eat all the guac."

Kerry blew out a breath and grabbed the bottle of wine, sloshing some into a glass. Who knew an innocent kiss on the cheek could get her so worked up?

Surely what she was feeling wasn't one-sided.

God, she hoped it wasn't. Taking a hearty sip of wine, she sank into the cushions. Tonight was going to be one hell of a date. And she couldn't wait to see what happened.

Chapter Seventeen

STARING INTO A hot oven did nothing to cool the fire flowing through him.

The second he'd spied Kerry standing in the doorway at her place, looking more beautiful than he ever thought possible, his body had been at half mast, and kissing her cheek pushed him to full mast.

And it's not like he really needed the approval from Kerry's father. The only approval he was truly after was from the woman in the living room. After the way her body swayed toward him just moments ago, he had an idea she wouldn't be averse to taking their relationship to the next level.

But first, he planned to get through dinner. The decision to eat at home was a risky one, but he just wanted it to be the two of them. With no waiters interrupting their conversation.

Cooking wasn't one of his greatest skills, but he could follow a recipe, or watch a YouTube video. Tonight he hadn't needed either for his roast chicken with vegetables. The meal his father always prepared for him when he returned from deployment. He liked to believe Dad would be happy with his retirement decision. He missed his dad. He would love it if Dad was still around so he could talk to him about what he'd decided but life didn't work out that way. Making this meal for Kerry seemed like the perfect way to pay tribute to the tradition his dad had started and the beginning of a new future. A new future with a new career and with Kerry by his side.

"Does it look like we need to be ordering pizza?"

Caleb startled, and the oven door slipped out of his hand, slamming shut. "Pizza?" he asked. "Oh, no, I haven't burned it. But the vegetables need about another ten minutes."

"Well, that's good to know." She sniffed and her nose scrunched cutely. "It does smell delicious. Are you going to tell me what we're having?"

"Nope." He wandered over to the fridge, the rush of cool air a welcome reprieve from the warmth of the oven and the desire flooding him. "You'll have to wait until I serve it to you."

"Ohh, I'm intrigued."

He chuckled as he pulled some water from the fridge, closing it with his hip. "It's nothing exotic. But it's—it has meaning to me."

"Then I'm sure it's going to be wonderful."

"I DON'T THINK I can eat another mouthful. That was delicious, Caleb."

He swallowed and smiled. "I'm glad you enjoyed it. It didn't turn out too bad, if I do say so myself."

"You say that like this is the first time you've cooked a roast dinner."

He fiddled with his beer bottle. "It's a meal I've had numerous times. This is the first time I've cooked it though. Usually my dad does."

"Oh, where is your dad? This is the first time you've mentioned him. Does he live in another state?"

"No. He died a year ago."

"Oh, Caleb, I'm so sorry."

He reached across the table and took hold of her hand that rested by her plate. "It's okay, you didn't know. How about we go into the living room and let dinner settle before we have some dessert?"

The questions she wanted to ask were shining in her eyes. The subject of his father's death wasn't one he spoke to many people about. He'd told the therapist he'd been made to see after his accident. He probably should've continued going, but after the required amount of sessions, the last thing he wanted to do was talk about his feelings and relive his dad's death as well as Trigger's.

"Sure, that sounds great."

Kerry extracted her hand, and he wanted to grab it again, keeping their connection.

Her chair scraped across the tile, and he copied her action, standing and stretching, working out the kink in his leg from sitting for too long at his small dinner table. "Hey, there's no need to do that," he protested when she started to collect the dirty plates.

"It's the least I could do after you made such a lovely meal."

No way was he going to let her do all the cleanup. He'd invited her over, and besides, the dishes could wait. He reached out and took them from her when she tried to brush past him. "I've got it, but thank you."

In seconds, he had the dishes piled on the side of the sink and faced Kerry, her gaze going from him to the dirty dishes. "What?" he asked at her.

"Aren't you going to put them in the dishwasher or at least rinse them?"

"Nope." He cupped her elbow and steered out into the hallway. "They're not going anywhere. They can stay where they are."

"But—"

He placed a finger over her lips. "Seriously, Kerry, I'd much rather spend time with you than worry about some dishes."

He pulled her into his arms, his hands resting on her hips. He lowered his head and captured her lips with his. A sigh of completion flowed through him. Nothing had ever felt as good as having Kerry in his arms.

He traced the seam of her lips with his tongue, and she opened up to let him in. A low moan came from her and her fingers dug into his chest where they were squashed between them.

His body flared to life and he pulled her closer to him, not bothering to hide his reaction to their kiss. Instead of pulling away, Kerry ground her hips against his hard flesh.

Back in the day, when all he wanted was to forget for a little while, he'd sweep the girl he was with into the bedroom and have her undressed in double-quick time. He hadn't taken advantage of them—they were with him all the way. In fact, most of the time they had his shirt off before he'd managed to unzip their dresses.

But the last thing he wanted to do was treat Kerry that way. At almost thirty-eight, he'd reached the conclusion he wouldn't have what the other guys on base, who had found their Mrs. Right, had. Now, he was hoping and praying the woman in his arms wanted a future with him, because with every passing second he held her, he never wanted to let her go.

The thought should frighten the hell out of him, but instead it empowered him. He dragged his lips against hers. Trailed hot kisses along her jawline until he found her ear. "Is this what you want, Kerry?"

"Yes. Yes, I want it all."

Bending his knees, putting most of his weight on his right leg, he scooped her up in his arms and carried her the short distance to his bedroom. Once beyond the threshold, he slid her down his body, framed her face with his hands, and reacquainted himself with her lips.

The hunger to have her settled into a pleasant buzz. She'd agreed to take the next step, and he planned to show her that she wouldn't regret this decision. Tonight he was going to worship the woman who'd come to mean so much to him.

ONE SECOND THEY were joking in the kitchen about dirty dishes and now she was in Caleb's room, his lips on hers and they were about to make love.

"Everything okay?" he whispered as his fingers played with the zipper tab of her dress.

"Yes, more than okay," she responded and began to unbutton his shirt. No way was she going to let anything overwhelm her in this moment. It was all about her and Caleb.

Sure, there were so many questions between them. She wanted to know about his father and how Caleb truly felt about retiring, but those things, like he'd said about the dirty dishes, weren't, going away. She wanted to remember every single second of making love together for the first time.

She pushed Caleb's shirt off his shoulders and her breath caught. She'd seen him bare chested before, but now she could touch the lightly tanned, muscular flesh. Run her fingers over the ridges; follow the trail with her tongue.

There was so much she wanted to do to him that once was definitely not going to be enough. As much as she wanted to, she couldn't suppress a seed of hope from sprouting inside of her. Hope that this was the beginning of a future with Caleb.

With him, she could be herself. She didn't have to be on show, a person she'd been molded and expected to be, like with her ex. With Caleb, she knew without a doubt that he would let her fly and be waiting without recrimination when she returned home.

Cool air whispered across her bare back from the air conditioner when he pulled her zipper down. She shrugged out of her dress, and the material bunched between their bodies. A shiver rippled through her as he brushed his lips across the top of her breasts.

She wanted more. Wanted him to release them from the confines of her bra. Wanted to feel his lips enclose around her nipple and suck.

"More, Caleb. I need more. I want everything."

"Never let it be said I don't listen." He took a step away from her, allowing her dress to fall to the ground. She watched as he quickly dealt with his trousers and underwear before standing in front of her naked and unashamed of his blatant desire for her.

Her mouth went dry at the beautiful specimen of a man

before her. There were a couple of scars, and she planned on asking him about them. She wanted to know everything about him. Later though. Now, all she wanted was to lose herself in his arms. Give herself over to being with someone who wanted to be with her. It had been so long since she'd been intimate with anyone; Winthorn had left her bed long ago. That should've been a big hint that things weren't what she thought they were, but she'd been so relieved that he didn't want her attention all of the time, she'd accepted it without explanation.

Warm hands closed over her shoulders, pulling her from the memories of her ex. Caleb's bedroom was the last place she needed to be having those thoughts. He pulled her close, and his erection butted up against her belly.

His fingers threaded through her hair, pulling gently so her head tipped back. His gaze met hers, a fire burning in their depths. She did this to him. She made him hard.

Never before had she experienced this type of empowerment. It was a heady sensation and one she could easily get used to.

Taking a step away from him, she reached behind her and unclasped her bra, shaking the lace and satin material from her arms. Next she hooked her fingers into the waistband of her panties, sliding them down her legs before kicking them away.

"You are so beautiful," he said as if she were a goddess. With Caleb looking at her, she did feel beautiful.

Needing to have his strong arms around her, she closed the distance she'd created and rubbed herself against him. "I'm all yours."

"Excellent." He smiled and then lowered his head to capture her lips once again. His hands roamed down her back until he reached her ass. She raised her leg and hooked it around his, angling her hips a little more against his erection, letting him know exactly what she wanted and where she wanted it.

Once again, he scooped her up in his arms and carried her over to the bed. The scent of fresh linen and his citrus aftershave mingled and surrounded her when he laid her on the mattress.

She dug her fingernails in his shoulders when he began to massage her breasts. Her body arched, giving him more access. His thumb brushed her engorged nipple, and a rush of warmth coalesced between her thighs.

His mouth replaced his hand and she moaned long and low. "Feels so good."

"There's more where this came from, trust me."

"Oh, I do." And she did.

Without a shadow of a doubt, she believed Caleb. He didn't seem the type to only go after his own pleasure like he who would not be named had been.

As much as she wanted to explore Caleb's body, she allowed him to learn what she liked. There was plenty of time for her to learn what he liked.

He kissed her again as his hand caressed her hip before sliding between her legs. She moved them apart to give him better access. He slid a finger inside of her and she shuddered. His thumb caressed her clit, enhancing the sensations flowing through her like a waterfall. He stroked in and out, adding another finger to increase her pleasure.

She tore her mouth away from his and drew in a deep breath, rocking her hips in time with the motion of his fingers. The tips of her toes began to tingle, moving up her legs until it reached the point where Caleb's tongue had joined his fingers.

She couldn't think; her mind was buzzing and her body wasn't far behind. The tingling between her legs spread wide, and her orgasm crashed over her. She bucked her hips against his fingers and mouth, wanting to draw out her release.

Caleb kissed his way back up her body, swirling his tongue around her nipple before biting it, causing another tremor. His erection rested on her thigh and, even though she'd experienced an amazing orgasm, she was more than ready to have him make love to her fully.

She framed his face and held it still so that she could kiss him. Her tongue delved in and his tongue met hers. Her hips lifted; she was far from done. As if understanding her silent message, Caleb swiveled his hips, and she groaned at the friction.

"I can't wait any longer. Take me, Caleb. Make me yours."

"Definitely." He rolled off her and she mourned the loss. A second later she heard the sound of the drawer opening and the distinctive crinkle of a condom. She would've offered to help him put it on, but he was back on top of her before she could catch her breath.

He positioned himself so their lower bodies were aligned. Kerry spread her legs.

Caleb slid an arm beneath her back, angling her.

Time stood still as she gazed into his eyes. The unspoken question hung in the air. Was she ready?

Her answer? She reached down and closed her fingers around his hard length, stroking from base to tip before guiding him to her entrance. He slowly entered her. She sighed in contentment when he filled her completely.

Their lips meshed together again, and Caleb withdrew slowly before plunging back in. Without thought, she lifted her hips, taking all of him. They repeated the action a few times before the heat began to rebuild inside of her. She dug her nails into Caleb's ass.

"Oh, yes, faster. Harder."

Caleb heeded her requests and, like before, all thoughts disappeared from her mind and all she concentrated on was the man above her and what he was doing to her body. Waves of pleasure built, waiting for the moment when everything would cease to exist and her orgasm would sweep her away. She didn't have to wait long; Caleb's forceful strokes were hitting the spot, and her body tensed before she climaxed hard around him. He shouted out her name as he came inside of her.

Her inner muscles clenched and released him, making her orgasm last longer. Nothing existed but the man in her arms, and she couldn't be happier.

Chapter Eighteen

CALEB JOLTED AWAKE, his heart racing. It took him a few seconds to get his bearings, but the familiar shape of his dresser appeared as the haze across his eyes cleared.

"Are you okay?" Kerry's husky voice washed over him and the tension he'd woken with dissipated as quickly as a Texas winter.

"Yeah, just a bad dream."

Well, he thought it was a bad dream. He couldn't recall it though. Which was unusual. Whenever he'd had a nightmare the vivid images always stayed with him.

He was about to pull Kerry close when he heard a faint sound, like a stray branch scratching against the roof. He knew for a fact there were no overhanging branches on his property. Perhaps he'd just imagined it.

"Did you hear that?" Kerry asked. Okay, he didn't imagine it.

"Yeah."

"Do you know what it is?"

He sat and craned his head in an attempt to see if he could hear it again. There it was, a faint scratching but it was followed by a short, sharp bark.

Kerry gasped beside him. "Is that? No, not possible, you said you were going to fix the hole. It can't possibly be Willow."

Caleb chuckled and was grateful for the darkened room so Kerry couldn't see the way his cheeks were heating. "Umm, I still haven't fixed it."

"You haven't?"

Amazing how much he could discern from tone without the benefit of light. Everything in Kerry's two words pointed to disbelief. Another muffled bark, and he tossed the covers back and picked up his pants, sliding one leg in, and almost ended up on the ground when his injured leg buckled beneath his weight.

"Fuck." He rubbed a hand down his leg, massaging the twitching muscle.

"Are you okay? What happened?"

"Nothing," he ground out. God, he hated the weakness in his leg.

Caleb zipped up his pants carefully, seeing as he was going commando, and limped down the hallway. He reached the back door of the kitchen in time to hear her scratching at it again. The damn dog was looking at wrecking his door.

He pulled it open and the annoyance that been festering in him disappeared when he clapped eyes on Willow's happy doggy face as she plopped down on her furry butt. "You are one determined pup, aren't you?"

He bent down and lifted her up in his arms. She snuggled in as she always did. Slowly but surely, Willow had wormed her way into his heart, not to mention her owner. After tonight, he couldn't imagine going forward without Kerry by his side. But he was getting ahead of himself.

When he walked into the bedroom, Kerry sat up, tucking the sheet under her breasts. With the light on behind her, he could see the dusky outline of her nipples. His body immediately reacted to the memory of how her breasts felt in his hands. The way she tasted on his tongue. He wanted to explore that taste again.

"Willow, what are you doing, girl?"

The dog wiggled in his arms, eager to get down.

He placed Willow on the bed and chuckled when she scampered up to her owner. Contentment shook her body when Kerry began to scratch her belly.

"Can I ask you a favor?"

"Sure," he responded, enjoying seeing Kerry and Willow in his bed.

"I should send Dad a text to let him know where Willow is in case he wakes up and tries to go looking for her. Are you able to grab my phone out of my handbag?"

"Sure, where is it?"

"It's on the side table by your couch."

"I'll be right back." He left her talking to Willow while he fetched her phone.

This was a first; he'd been under the impression that a

woman's handbag was a sacrilegious item no man was ever allowed to look inside. It was exactly where she said it was going to be. He unzipped it and found the phone and something else he hadn't expected to see.

"Well, now, this is interesting." Palming the item and phone, he zipped up the bag and headed back to his room, a little spring in his step.

He paused in the doorway, admiring the view. Kerry had settled herself back on the pillows and Willow was snuggled up against her. Again, this vision was something he could definitely get used to.

His body stirred back to life and he deftly undid his trousers and let them fall to the floor. "I've got your phone."

Kerry looked up, a slow smile spreading across her face. "Hmm, that's not all you've got."

Her sultry comment only intensified his desire. He held up the condom he'd found. "So, I guess we can put this to good use?"

A slight pink hue crept up her cheeks. He chuckled.

"Well, you certainly look like you're up for the task. So how about it, solider? Ready for round two?"

He stalked toward the bed, ripping the square foil as he went. "That's airman, ma'am, not soldier. And I'm more than ready for round two."

KERRY LAY SNUGGLED against Caleb's chest one arm firmly around her back and his other hand was absently scratching Willow.

She didn't want to kill the post-sex relaxation mood they were in, but there were questions she wanted to ask him. Even though she'd come over to celebrate his retirement, they'd talked about everything but that over dinner. Not to mention the news he'd dropped on her about his father passing away. And then they'd skipped dessert for a different kind of sweet.

Now was as good a time as any. She took a deep breath and dove in. "We never did talk about what you're going to do now that you've decided to retire."

Lying so close to him, she couldn't miss his muscles tensing. Retiring had to have been a hard decision to make, but she'd seen the way his leg had crumpled beneath him when he'd gotten out of bed. Being a liability was the last thing Caleb would want to be.

"I've got a couple of options in mind. I need to speak to some people. I technically don't retire for another couple of months, so I don't have to make any rash decisions."

There was not a scrap of emotion in his voice, the words so matter-of-fact her heart hurt. No wonder Willow had latched onto him. She'd wanted to stop his hurting. And for some reason, he hadn't fixed the area where Willow could escape from her home into his yard.

That had to mean something, didn't it?

"I think whatever you do, you'll do it well." Now that he was being more open with her, she wanted to know more. Only this next question might bring the barriers slamming back down around him. She said a silent prayer that wouldn't be the outcome. "What happened to your dad? Was he sick?"

A shudder rippled through Caleb and Willow whimpered. Kerry glanced up in time to see him loosening his grip on Willow's fur. In all likelihood, he hadn't hurt her pet; it was more that Willow sensed his distress and she didn't like it.

"He died in a car accident. He was on his way to see me in the hospital."

Kerry swallowed against the lump forming in her throat and blinked her eyes a couple of times to prevent the tears from falling. How awful for him. So much to handle in such a short amount of time. When he needed someone to lean on and help him, he'd been left alone.

But he'd also said that his dad prepared the traditional meals.

"What about your mom? Where's she?"

Another sigh huffed out of him. "She and dad divorced when I was barely one. I hardly remember her. She was from England and so she moved back, remarried, and had another family. You can't miss what you've never had."

Wow, life hadn't been very fair to Caleb. No wonder he'd been so prickly when they'd first met.

The words *I'm sorry* were on the tip of her tongue, but, right now, she had an idea he didn't want to hear that phrase. Instead, she placed a kiss over his heart and laid her hand on top as if to keep the kiss from escaping into the air.

They lay there for a few moments, neither saying anything, the only sound being an occasional snore coming from Willow. Kerry would have to leave soon; she had the lunch shift today and had to pick up the cease-and-desist letter from the lawyer George had recommended. He'd phoned her back within two hours, stating that in Texas law Winthorn had no claim, and she had left everything behind anyhow. The lawyer could forward it to her ex by courier, but Kerry would rather hand deliver it. Then she'd know for sure he'd received the letter. She couldn't believe her problem could be solved so quickly and without her having to see her jerk of an ex.

"Who's Winthorn, and why is he asking you for money?"

Where had that come from? Oh, yes, Caleb had seen the letter. Now she didn't think she'd get away with avoiding the subject. Not after he'd shared details about his family.

God, talking about Winthorn was about as appealing as a root canal. Was there an etiquette rule about talking about an old lover while in bed with your new one?

Caleb's fingers brushed up and down her arm, giving her the silent support she'd given him.

If they had any chance of a future—and after spending

the night in his arms, she hoped like hell they did—she couldn't hide her past from him. Nothing good would come of it if she did.

"Winthorn was my ex. We were together for over seven years."

"Why is he saying you owe him money? Are these funds part of a divorce settlement or something?"

Kerry scoffed. "As if. I was never good enough to go from girlfriend to wife. I was simply a doll he played with and then when he decided I wasn't good enough he chucked me out."

She yelped as Caleb moved and she found herself on the sheets instead of resting against his chest.

"Sorry," he muttered and changed his position so he was curled around her. "What do you mean he chucked you out?"

She sighed. "It's best if I start at the beginning."

"Okay, but, Kerry…" He paused and she looked up at him, her heart skipping a beat when she saw longing, not pity, in his gaze, his chocolate-brown eyes so warm and welcoming. "Whatever you say won't change how I feel about you."

How she wanted to ask what he felt for her, but she didn't. And regardless of him saying that her story wouldn't change his thoughts, she couldn't help but think it might. Who would want to be with someone weak like her?

"Thank you," she said. Hopefully, her worries weren't

showing on her face. "I met Winthorn at the beginning of my third year of college. He was the cliché of college movies and novels. The rich, good-looking guy who could have any girl he wanted, but he picked me, the shy quiet girl who wasn't in any sorority and didn't have a lot of friends. Of course, I was flattered that the best guy in the senior class was interested in me. We dated that whole year and he treated me like a princess. I had visions of us marrying and having kids and the perfect life. He graduated and started working at his parents' investment firm in Dallas. We attended so many functions that I was missing a lot of classes. Winthorn encouraged me to leave school, said I didn't have to worry about anything because he would take care of me.

"Like the lovestruck girl I was, I gave up, much to my father's annoyance but my mom's delight. She was getting sicker with her MS, and all she wanted was to see me married to a wonderful man. In her eyes, Winthorn was that man. He was a man who could look after me. Mom was still a little old-fashioned and thought one of my jobs was to make my man happy and to create a beautiful home for him to come back to each night. It was never my dream to be a housewife, but between not wanting to disappoint my mom when I knew she was going to die and wanting to please Winthorn, it wasn't hard to give in to their ideals."

"I take it he wasn't." Caleb commented when she paused.

"No. Over time, he manipulated me so cleverly that I

didn't see it. He would come home with outfits for me, saying he loved shopping for me and wanted the best-dressed woman on his arm. Slowly, he overtook everything in my life. Told me how to get my hair cut. What to say when we went out, which, toward the end, was to keep my mouth shut and smile. Even then I didn't see what he was doing. Dad did and tried to tell me. Mom, at this time, was bedridden and still saw Winthorn as my white knight, so she would brush Dad's concerns away."

Pain stabbed her in the stomach. How stupid she'd been. But after today, it would be all over. When she delivered the letter she planned to tell her loser ex to stay out of her life— permanently.

"I'm sorry you went through that, honey. I can see you're beating yourself up about it, but you got out and, from what I can see, have taken back control of your own life. You should be proud of what you've accomplished."

"Well, it's only because he kicked me out when he'd decided I was no longer useful to him. I had nothing but the clothes I was wearing and sixty dollars in my wallet. I *didn't* walk away. I was shoved, and I had no choice but to pick up the pieces."

Caleb changed their positions again so he could face her, and placed his hands on her shoulders. Admiration shone in his eyes and her fear of rejection disappeared like a magician's coin. "But you did, and it doesn't matter how it happened. You could've collapsed in a heap or gone crawling back to him. I'm surprised that wasn't the outcome he wanted. I'm betting he hoped you'd realize you couldn't live without him and beg him to give you another chance. When you didn't, he waited until he deemed the time was right to disrupt your life again. And now is that time, seeing as you've got a house and steady income. Everything he held you back from achieving."

"I had the same thought. But anyway, I've got the situation under control, and when I'm finished with him, he will wish he'd never tried to extort money out of me."

"That's my girl."

She crawled over Caleb until she was straddling him, her hands resting on his chest. "I think we've done enough talking for one day." Against her butt she could feel his growing erection.

"I totally agree," he said and pulled her down for a kiss.

Everything about being with Caleb was different than when she was with Winthorn. The way he spoke to her, treated her, hell, even kissed her. With Caleb, everything seemed right, too right, and it scared the crap out of her. How could she trust her judgment when she'd been so wrong in the past?

Chapter Nineteen

T HERE WAS A lightness in Caleb's step as he opened the
door to the veteran's center. He'd received a call from
George while he was kissing Kerry goodbye.

He wondered if this meeting was about a couple of the
possible job opportunities they had discussed the other day.
He wasn't sure he was ready to make a decision today, but
listening wouldn't hurt.

After, he planned on visiting someone else, once he
found out a little more about Kerry's ex. It had taken
everything in him to keep his muscles relaxed while Kerry
relayed everything she'd been through with the jerk. She said
she was going to handle it, and he had no doubt that she
would, but it wouldn't hurt for him to visit the guy and tell
him that Kerry was his.

And she was. After this morning, he didn't want to be
alone anymore. He wanted to walk in on the sight of her and
Willow in his bed every morning. He hoped she felt the
same way. He had no doubt Willow would be happy with
the arrangement.

Damn, two months ago the idea of having another dog

in his life was abhorrent to him. Then a corgi had decided he needed rescuing, and she wasn't going to give up.

No, he couldn't totally give Willow all the credit. If it weren't for his attraction to Kerry, he would've fixed the hole in the fence, refused to help with Ron, and definitely refused to have dinner with her.

Kerry had given him his life back and he planned to do the same, after he'd seen George, of course.

She's not going to like you interfering.

He ignored the voice in his head.

He knocked on George's door, unconsciously straightening his spine like he did when he always entered his lieutenant colonel's office. Old habits died hard.

"Come in."

He opened the door and smiled when the other man waved him in, exactly like Blue used to do. "Hi, George."

"Caleb, glad you could make it. Now that you've made the decision to retire, I want to expand on the ideas I floated one of the times we chatted."

His stomach dropped. Going into the military had been his focus since high school. After his first year, he'd always pictured himself not retiring until he was in his sixties. Now the thought of a new career freaked him out a little, but he also couldn't stay at home all day twiddling his thumbs.

"What did you want to talk about?"

"As you're aware, a lot of therapy dogs come into the center. We've found over the last year, since we started the program, that the animals have helped our vets significantly."

"Right, what about it?"

"Well, the agency that trains the dogs is looking for someone to oversee their recruitment. The person in the position has decided to leave, like Bill alluded to when we were talking that day. I think this will be perfect for you. You've had experience with handling dogs and know what to look for."

A cold sweat broke out over his forehead. He could spend time with Willow because he was used to her, but to be surrounded by dogs day in and day out?

"I'm not sure that's a good fit for me."

George leaned forward and clasped his hands on top of the shiny desk. "Look, I understand what happened to you and your K-9 partner. I imagine it's difficult getting past knowing your friend basically sacrificed his life for yours. But, Caleb, this will be a good way to heal. You don't have to stay there forever, but as a job out of the air force, I think it will be a good fit. You wouldn't have stayed in the K-9 unit as long as you did, even knocking back offers for promotion, if you didn't love working with dogs. Think of this as easing your way back into civilian life."

He scoffed. "Easing my way in by working with the one animal that it still hurts to be around? I'm really not sure about this, George."

"I get your reluctance, I really do, but I want you to think about it. Think about all the ex-servicemen you're going to help. You never know, it might be therapeutic for you. I've seen what Willow and Kerry have done for you."

He sat a little straighter, surprised at George's observation. "What do you mean?"

"One of the first times you came in, you did everything you could to ignore Willow. You wanted to get out of this place faster than a solider seeking shelter from a gun-toting terrorist. You also kept sneaking glances to where Kerry was. And I've seen you two together a lot since that game night.

"Slowly, I've seen you become more relaxed around Willow, too, I'm not sure you're aware of it, but when she's near you, you visibly relax and you automatically pat her."

Caleb let George's words sink in. Everything he'd said was true—hadn't he just admitted to himself earlier how important Kerry and Willow were to him?

Hell, he was falling in love with Kerry, and that wouldn't have happened if it weren't for a therapy dog.

In love?

The thought should scare him, but it didn't. Joy and a sense of calmness settled in him. Could he do this? Could he spend his time around dogs?

Yes.

It would be a way he could honor Trigger and the importance of what he'd done when they'd been a team and the sacrifice he'd made for him.

"Yes, I'll talk to them."

George beamed. "Excellent. They'll be so happy. I had

thought about getting you involved in some way here, but I think this will work out better. Besides, I'm sure I'll be seeing a lot of you anyway. Now let me see where I put the contact details."

He shuffled some papers and Caleb pulled out his phone and searched Winthorn Hartigan the third. Now that this meeting was over, it was on to the next one.

Two hours after his meeting with George, he stared at another door. This time it wasn't nerves beating their drum in his belly; it was anger on behalf of Kerry. The worst thing he could do was charge in there, guns blazing. He needed to be cool and calm. In control of his emotions and his words.

"Are you planning on standing there all day, buddy? If you don't move, I'll call the police and get you removed."

Caleb had just found who he was looking for, if his tone and threat was anything to go by. He turned and the man behind him fit every preconceived idea he had of a pretentious asshole. His hair was coifed in a style that screamed *I come from money*. And even though Caleb had a few inches on him, the other man still managed to look down his nose at him.

"Winthorn Hartigan the third, I take it," he commented, trying to keep the anger out of his tone.

"Who's asking?"

That was as good as admitting who he was.

"Caleb Bradshaw, a friend of Kerry Williams. I'm here about the letter you sent her."

Winthorn's eyebrows rose. "A friend of Kerry's?" Then he laughed, and Caleb thrust his hands in his pockets to stop himself from punching this guy out. "Oh, this is rich. She sends a lackey to come see me because she's too scared."

Polite wasn't going to cut it with the guy. Caleb stepped up to him so that there was barely an inch between them. "Listen here, asshole. Kerry didn't send me. I found you and came to see you myself. But I will say that when you threaten Kerry, you're threatening me. So take this is as a warning—I know you think you have a monetary claim over her, but I'm telling you, you need to back off."

"Or what? What are you going to do? Drag me through court? Because, let me tell you, I have the financial means to drag this out for a very long time."

"If you're so well off, why do you need to go after Kerry?"

For a second, a flicker of doubt entered Winthorn's eyes. "You don't need to know. Is that all? Because, unlike you, I have work to do."

He shoved past Caleb and into the building. Once the door shut, Caleb ran his fingers through his hair. That hadn't gone the way he wanted it to. Somehow, he had a feeling he'd made things worse for Kerry instead of better.

Dammit, he should've listened to the voice in his head that told him this was a bad idea.

IT WAS CLOSE to five by the time she arrived at Winthorn's office, and she hoped he hadn't decided to leave early. He hadn't usually when they were together, but who knew now?

She rushed through the door and practically slammed into the reception desk. "Hi, I want to see Winthorn, please." She huffed the words, but they sounded strong.

And please don't give me a hard time. I just want this meeting over and done with.

"Do you have an appointment?"

"No, but I know he'll want to see me. Tell him Kerry Williams is here."

"Mr. Hartigan is a very busy man; he doesn't have time to see people who just drop in unannounced."

Her snooty voice was annoying, and Kerry cast her eyes to the ceiling and counted to ten. Once she felt she had herself under some sort of control, she pasted a smile on her face. "Look, I know just how busy Winthorn can be. I lived with him for quite a number of years. I also know that he won't have any appointments this close to five. So please inform Mr. Hartigan the third that Kerry Williams is here to see him. Thank you."

The woman eyed her for a few seconds before picking up the phone and speaking quietly into it.

"Mr. Hartigan said he'd see you. If you'd like to go to the conference room, he'll meet you there. It's the second door on the right down that hallway." She pointed as she spoke.

Kerry had no doubt if it were anyone else to see Winthorn, they'd be escorted to the room and not have to make their own way.

"Thank you." She tightened her grip on her purse, paranoid that somehow the letter from the solicitor would disappear. She made her way to where she'd been directed and stepped into the large space. Walking over to the window, she gazed out into the streetscape below. People were bustling along the sidewalk, heading for their cars or maybe to a bar to meet friends for after-work drinks. It may be a Wednesday night and hump day, but she knew, from the patronage at the restaurant, people began the count down to the weekend.

The door slammed and she jumped, whirling around to see her ex standing, arms crossed and a thunderous look on his face.

"What do you want, Kerry? Come to finish what your lackey started earlier?" He practically spat out the word.

She'd never thought her ex would hurt her, but she took a step back now and her right hip connected with the credenza against the wall.

"I-I've c-come." She stopped and pushed away her fear. She was stronger than this. If he laid a finger on her, she'd press charges. Once it got out that one of Dallas's elites had hit a woman, the press would be all over him. She'd then bring up everything he'd done to her. Raking his name through the mud would give her a lot of pleasure.

She stepped away from where she cowered and lifted her chin. "I've come to give you a letter from my solicitor. The letter states that you have no right to demand any sort of payment from me. Under Texas law, we weren't ever married, simply roommates with the odd benefit."

"You're feeling brave now that your *boyfriend* came to see me, are you?" he sneered, completely ignoring her claim.

But his words made no sense. She didn't have a boyfriend. Well, she supposed she had a lover, but she and Caleb hadn't discussed their relationship status. And she was certain Caleb wouldn't come and see Winthorn, not without telling her.

"I have no idea what you're talking about. All I'm here for is to give you this cease-and-desist letter and leave."

"Does the name Caleb Bradshaw ring a bell?"

Kerry couldn't stop the gasp from escaping. Caleb had been here to see him? No, she didn't believe Winthorn. But what choice did she have? No way could the jerk have pulled Caleb's name out of thin air.

Her simmering anger welled up inside of her, threatening to spew in the direction of both Winthorn and Caleb.

Why did the men she fell in love with think she was incapable of running her own life?

Granted, she'd been young and stupid and had let Winthorn take over. Caleb, though, after how he'd said last night that she was brave and strong, how could he go behind her back and warn off Winthorn?

"I see that the name does. His words don't mean anything to me, but give me the letter from your solicitor." He held his hand out, fluttering his fingers in annoyance.

Opening her purse, she pulled out the letter, gripping it in her hand. "Before I hand this over to you, I want you to understand one thing, Winthorn."

"What's that?"

She waved the letter. "My solicitor looked over your letter. Listened to everything I had to say. His opinion is attached. You have no leg to stand on, and the fact you expect me to pay you back when I *never* asked for anything is ridiculous." He opened his mouth to say something but she didn't give him a chance. "I never wanted you for your money. If you recall, I wanted to get a job, but you didn't want me to. You wanted to control every aspect of my life. You used emotional abuse to keep me by your side.

"Well, I'm telling you now, you have no control over me anymore. And you are not going to get your grubby little hands on anything of mine. The day you kicked me out was the best day of my life. If you ever try to come after me again, I will make sure everyone knows just what a controlling asshole you truly are." She tossed the letter on the table, ignoring his still outstretched hand. "Goodbye, Winthorn. I never want to see you again."

She stormed past him and didn't pause until she was half a block away from his building. Only then did she stop and wrap her arms around her middle. Her breath sawed in and out, and her heart beat out of her chest.

She'd done it. She'd stood up to Winthorn and it felt amazing. She had no idea if he would try to come after her again, but she suspected he wouldn't. This had been a test to see if she'd crawl back to him. If she'd still be that yes girl he'd known. Well, now he knew. She wasn't, and if he did try anything again, well, she'd be more than willing to play dirty.

Now that the adrenaline of facing her slimy ex had settled down, part of the encounter came back to her.

Caleb had gone to see Winthorn.

He'd gone behind her back, believing she was incapable of handling the situation, even though she told him she had it all under control.

Just when she was beginning to trust him, he'd betrayed her by taking command of her life. Well, she wasn't going to stand for it. She wasn't going to fall into the trap of having a man take over her life. She couldn't trust Caleb now. Couldn't trust that this wasn't the start of the long walk down the road she'd sworn she'd never travel again.

To save herself, she had to walk away now.

Her heart might break in the process, but she'd survive. She'd come back from being broken once, and she could do it again.

Only this time the hurt cut deeper.

Chapter Twenty

CALEB PACED HIS living room, stopping every now and then to gaze out the front window to see if Kerry's car was in her driveway.

After returning from his meeting with Winthorn, he'd gone down to the local gym where he worked off his anger. He was doing his bench presses when it hit him. He'd done exactly what the asshole had done to Kerry for most of their relationship—taken over. He'd taken a liberty he had no right to take by visiting Kerry's loser ex.

The Kerry he was familiar with was more than capable of dealing with whatever her ex was doing to her. He should've left it alone and just been there as a support for her.

A loud pounding echoed through the house—his time had run out. He only hoped that if he apologized enough, she'd forgive him and give him a second chance.

That was the only option he was allowing himself to think about. Any other option, such as she said she wanted nothing to do with him, he didn't want to contemplate.

"Open the door, Caleb Bradshaw. I know you're in there."

Yep, he'd fucked it up badly.

Never one to back down from a fight—hell, as an airman he had no choice but to face untenable situations—he'd face this one head-on. Just because he planned to retire didn't mean he'd lost any of the strength and resolve that had been drummed into him during the last twenty years.

He opened the door and she marched right in. In another circumstance, he might have smiled at her bravado. But this was not the time for smiling.

She stood silhouetted by the living room window, still wearing her smart black trousers and white blouse. Her hair was out of the ponytail she'd put it in for work and it looked knotted, as if she'd been winding it around her fingers.

He wanted to pull her into his arms and hold her while he said sorry over and over. Her back was ramrod straight; any attempt by him to touch her would be slapped away.

As if sensing his presence, she whirled around, hurt and betrayal shining brightly in her eyes. Not the emotions he wanted to elicit from her.

"Before you say anything, please let me apologize. I'm so sorry, Kerry, I fucked up badly. I interfered when I shouldn't have. Can you forgive me?"

She wrapped her arms around her belly, holding in the pain, and hope died a little. "No, Caleb, I can't. You crossed a line, and that's unforgiveable to me."

The rest of his hope blew up in flames, leaving nothing but a hollow shell. He'd thought losing Trigger was hard, but knowing he'd lost the only woman he'd ever loved devastated him, crushing his heart in way not even the visit from the police on the night of his father's death had done.

But he wouldn't give up. Not now. Not when he'd found the person who made him whole.

"Are you sure? Is there nothing I can say that will make you change your mind?"

She shook her head. "Do you know what you did to me by going to see Winthorn?"

Yes, he knew, but he couldn't form the right words to say it.

"Caleb, you treated me exactly like Winthorn did throughout our entire relationship. You took control of the situation because you believed I couldn't. You believed I was too weak to be able to deal with his threat. He wasn't coming after you; he was coming after *me*. It wasn't your problem to take on. And by doing so, I don't think I can ever trust you again.

"Once I clawed my way back from the lowest point of my life, I vowed that I would never let a man control any aspect of my life ever again. And I thought you understood that. I thought you saw me for the person I've become. You even said the words. You said I was strong and independent. But they were just platitudes. Deep down, you think I'm weak."

"No," he burst out. He closed the distance between them. The need to touch her was strong, but he shoved his hands into his pants pockets. "I never thought that of you. You are strong and independent. It's what I love about you."

"Stop it. Don't say that word to me. You can't love me if you acted the way you did. That's not love, Caleb. That's control. And I've had it once in my life. I'm not having it again." She stepped away from him, and his heart shattered until there was nothing left but a small pile of fragments he didn't believe would ever be whole again. He watched helplessly as she walked away from him.

He followed her into the hallway but stopped a few feet from where she stood by his front door. Did she stop because she'd changed her mind? No, that was wishful thinking on his part. Her spine was straighter than his had ever been during a parade. Her resolve to leave hadn't wavered, and even though she was ripping him to shreds, the way she was standing up for herself right now only deepened his love for her.

She looked him in the eye, tears shimmering from hers in the golden light from the chandelier. "I'd appreciate it if you would fix the fence so Willow can't come into your yard. I think it would be best if we cut all ties." She gripped the door handle. "Goodbye, Caleb."

This wasn't goodbye. Yes, he'd fucked up hugely, but he wanted Kerry and Willow in his life for forever.

And he was going to make it happen.

DON'T LOOK OVER. Don't look over.

Willow pulled at her lead, trying to get her to change direction to head next door and not into her car.

It had been three long weeks since she'd walked out of Caleb's house. Three weeks where her emotions had ranged from anger to sadness. And underneath it all, one emotion never changed and that was the love she felt for Caleb.

What she had gone through emotionally when Winthorn had kicked her out with nowhere to go was nothing compared to the void that kept her company now. Dad was constantly on her back, telling her to go over and talk to Caleb, that the basis of a good relationship was communication and the second people stopped talking everything fell apart.

In her heart, she knew her dad was right, but her logic was cautioning her to protect herself. If Caleb could take over once, he could take over her life again. All the little things built up until there was a mountain and she was stuck at the bottom, struggling to climb up when she should be waving her achievement flag at the summit.

Trust was another major factor in a relationship. If there wasn't trust, what hope was there?

Willow barked and Kerry looked up, her gaze connecting with Caleb's.

Damn the man. He looked sexy in his tight, white T-shirt and blue jeans. The sun hit his brown hair at just the right angle, highlighting the golden strands in it. He'd had it cut some time in the last three weeks. If she thought he looked sexy with long, shaggy hair, he looked even hotter with a short back and sides cut. From the distance between them, she couldn't make out the look in his eyes, but she imagined it was warm and enticing like before he kissed her.

Willow tugged hard on her lead and Kerry took a step forward, but then her mind overruled her heart and she stopped. Instead, she nodded at him and turned her back, walking to her car as quickly as she could, ignoring Willow's bark and continual pulling on the lead.

Once she settled Willow and herself, she gripped the steering wheel and let out a long, cleansing breath. A glance in her rearview mirror showed an empty space—Caleb had left, and the realization hurt more than she ever thought it could.

Kerry laid her head on her hands. She counted to five, and once she felt in control again, lifted her head, rolled her shoulders, and looked in the rearview mirror. "Oh, Willow, what am I going to do?"

The dog remained silent but had a reproachful look in her eyes.

THREE HOURS LATER, Kerry opened the door to the veteran's center and released Willow from her lead. As her pet trotted down the hallway, her furry butt swaying sassily from side to side, a bit of peace entered Kerry's soul.

She liked coming to the center. Liked knowing every time she and Willow visited, they brightened someone's day and chased the shadows away from their soul.

George had mentioned that today the organization she'd done her training through was visiting. She was looking forward to seeing Bill again.

The buzz from the main room seemed a little louder and... wait? Was that Willow barking excitedly? Oh no, that couldn't be good. Willow was meant to be a calming influence, not an excitable one, and it was so out of character for her to act this way.

Kerry hurried into the room, not looking where she was going, and slammed right into a hard body holding something furry.

She breathed deeply in an attempt to get herself under control and was assailed by a very familiar citrus scent.

"Caleb?" she asked as she looked up into dreamy chocolate eyes. "What are you doing here?"

He didn't say anything but put Willow on the ground, patted her head, and then grabbed Kerry's hand.

She had no choice but to follow him out of the room.

"Where are we going?" she asked, finally finding her voice. She started to tug her hand away but stopped. It was so good to have skin on skin contact with him. Her body warmed, and she hadn't even realized she'd been cold.

Caleb strode through the hall with purpose until he ushered them into George's office. "Why are we here?" she asked. "I need to go back out there. Check on Willow."

He still had hold of her hand and brought it up to his lips. "I'm sorry, Kerry, so sorry for what I did."

Her heart screamed at her to jump into his arms and kiss his face all over, while yelling, *It's okay. I forgive you. I love you.*

Dammit, the last bit of her thought was true. She did love Caleb. Hadn't stopped in the time they'd been apart.

But there was still the problem of trust. He had to show her an awful lot to convince her that he would take her trust and look after it.

Kerry pulled her hands away, missing their connection straightaway. "You said that to me three weeks ago, too. I believe you are sorry, Caleb, and I want to forgive you, but I'm not sure I can."

His shoulders slumped for a second before he straightened them again. Determination flared in his eyes and she found herself moving toward him, not away. "I know what I did was the worst possible thing I could've done. I treated you in a way you didn't deserve to be treated."

She couldn't deny his sincerity, but sincerity wasn't a guarantee it wouldn't happen again. "As I said, I don't doubt that you're sorry. What I want to know is why. Why did you do it? Did you think I couldn't handle Winthorn?"

"No." The word burst out of him. "I never doubted for a minute that you could handle him. You walked away and put your life back together. You *are* a strong woman."

"You're right. I am, so why did you interfere?"

Her heart dipped. He appeared to be struggling to form a reasonable explanation. Was he coming up with a lie to give her?

She turned her back and gazed, unseeing, at George's desk. She should walk out, but she was mourning the fact that being strong didn't mean she couldn't be hurt.

I'M FUCKING THIS up.

The words twisted through his mind like a roller coaster. Everything he was saying was coming out wrong. It sounded smart in his head, but when he said it out loud, it came out the opposite of what he wanted.

If he didn't answer soon, she was going to open that door and disappear, this time for good? He could feel it in his bones, and he couldn't let that happen.

He had to go with the truth. Just throw out why he did it and hoped like hell she believed him.

"It's simple—I did it because I love you. He was hurting you and because you mean the world to me, he was hurting me too."

She whirled around, her beautiful hazel eyes wide. Well, at least that got a reaction from her.

Seeing it as a positive sign, he approached her again. Everything in him wanted to bring her close. To inhale the fresh scent of apple from her shampoo. She fit perfectly in his arms, in his bed, and in his life.

He gave in to his desires and stroked a hand down her hair, twirling one of the strands around his finger before releasing it. "What I should've done was volunteer to come with you. Be your silent support and let you deal with it in your way. I believe you can handle anything that's thrown at you. You told me you had the situation sorted and I should've listened."

The silence stretched between them. Had he left it too long? Should he have gone over to her place and demanded she see him? No, that would've made it even worse. He'd been all types of stupid and he would have to pay the price. Whatever that was.

"Yes," she whispered. "That's exactly what you should've done."

Energy flowed through him. Maybe, just maybe, the second chance he wanted was within his grasp. "I want a future with you and Willow. I want to come home to you every day, and I want to listen as you tell me about your troubles. I want to make a life with you. I love you, Kerry. You and your dog changed my life, and I don't want to go back to the man I was before we met. Can we please try again?"

Tears shimmered in her eyes, and he didn't know what he'd do if they spilled over. Well, he'd hold her close and let her cry, be the silent support she needed and the support he said he'd be for her.

A pair of arms slipped around his waist, and his breath shuddered out of him as he wrapped her tightly against him. "I didn't know how much I needed you until you stumbled into my arms. That day was the best day of my life."

She pulled back and he gently wiped the tears away from her cheeks.

"It was the best day of my life, too."

His eyes drifted shut as fingers trailed a sweet path down his cheek, and he pursed his lips when they brushed them. "Look at me, Caleb."

He opened his eyes, gazing down at the woman in his arms. The woman he loved with all his heart. The woman who'd reminded him that to live was to love.

"I love you, too, Caleb Bradshaw. Promise me you won't ever try to take over my life again."

He pressed his lips softly against hers. "I promise. I'll be your shoulder when you need it. The person who will stand at your side when you need it. But if you're physically threatened, I'm going to act. No one *hurts* what's mine. And you're mine, Kerry Williams. All mine."

"I like the sound of that."

Epilogue

KERRY SHOOK HER head at the boxes stacked in her living room. "Where the hell are we going to fit all this stuff?"

A set of warm lips landed on the back of her neck, startling her. "Don't worry, honey, we'll find a place. If not, we can toss it and start over buying stuff that's *ours*."

She whirled around and flung her arms around Caleb's shoulders. "I like the sound of ours."

Two months had passed since the day in George's office. Caleb had told her all about his new position where he would be overseeing the acquiring and training of the therapy dogs and she couldn't be more excited for him. The lease on his place was up, and it made more sense for him to move in with her, seeing as he spent most of his time at her place anyway.

Her dad had recovered and was back living in his apartment. He'd found a lady friend who had recently moved in and was spending all his time with Paula. Kerry liked her and seeing her dad with a spring in his step lightened her heart.

"I can't believe this is finally happening," she said.

"Believe it. But it's not like this is really anything different to what we've been doing for the last two months."

"Very true. Oh, did you fix the hole in the fence? We don't want Willow escaping next door now that you're not there." Something the dog had done on numerous occasions when Caleb had gone to his place for any given amount of time. It was another reason why he'd been spending most of his time in her house.

"I did. There will be no more escape attempts."

"My next-door knight," she joked before pouring all her love for him into a kiss. His arms tightened around her and he deepened the kiss.

"Get a room, you two."

A voice broke into their bubble, and Kerry went up on tiptoe to look over Caleb's shoulder. His former roommate Ethan stood in the doorway of the living room, with a big grin on his face, a case of beer in one hand and an arm around his fiancée, Isabella, and their daughter, Marnie.

"You're not supposed to be here for another hour, Ethan," Caleb grumbled as he dropped a kiss on her nose before releasing her.

"Thought we'd come and help." Ethan held up the case of beer. "Point me to the kitchen and I'll dump this and then help you unpack or haul furniture. Whatever you both need."

"The kitchen's this way."

Kerry tracked Caleb's movement out of the room, admir-

NICOLE FLOCKTON

ing the curve of his ass in his jeans. Willow, being Willow, trotted after Caleb, always wanting to be near him as much as Kerry did.

"Thank you," Isabella said quietly.

"What?" she asked.

"Thank you for bringing back Caleb. When I first met him he was in a dark place. He only came out when the guys pressured him and, well, let's just say his choice of company wasn't the best. But when he met you, I've never seen a man change so much. You're good for him."

"He's good for me too," she said simply. "We bring out the best in each other."

"Yes, you do. Oh, I can't wait for you to meet my friend, Meredith. She's coming back to town in a few weeks after her stint overseas."

"Is she military?"

"Oh no, she's a schoolteacher like me, or I was until I had Marnie. But she's been teaching overseas for almost a year. A great opportunity knocked and she answered. I think the two of you will get on well."

"I'll look forward to meeting her. Is she married or single?"

"Very much single. Meredith likes walking to her own beat. But I would like to see her settle down one day."

The men returned and Caleb was shaking his head.

"What's wrong?" she rushed up to her man.

"I was just telling Caleb that our friend, Linc, has left the army," Ethan commented.

"And I take it that's a bad thing?"

Caleb shrugged. "No, not really, more of a shock. We all thought he would be career army."

"Well, he has his reasons, I'm sure, just like you did." She drew Caleb into her arms. No sooner had her fingers locked together against his back than Willow barked.

"Needy baby, greedy baby," she groused as she released her hold on Caleb and picked up the dog.

She looked closer at the dog and spied a blue ribbon hanging from her collar with something attached to it. That something sparkled. She looked up at Caleb, love shining brightly in his eyes.

"What's going on?" she asked as he gathered her close.

"Kerry Williams, the day a little dog waddled into my yard was the best day of my life. It seemed only fitting to have her be a part of this moment." He reached over and pulled the ribbon; the ring slid off and he got down on one knee.

"Will you marry me?"

He held the ring up and tears filled Kerry's eyes. She hugged Willow then placed her on the ground before dropping to her knees. "Yes, Caleb Bradshaw. Yes, I will marry you."

He slid the ring home and, before she could admire it, pulled her close for a kiss. She was vaguely aware of clapping in the background.

She pulled away from him and looked over her shoulder to see Ethan and Isabella smiling at them.

Willow squeezed under her arms and placed herself between the two of them, clearly happy with both her humans. Caleb smiled and scratched Willow's head, but his eyes were firmly on Kerry's.

"Mine," he said.

Kerry smiled. "Ours, forever."

The End

Acknowledgements

A huge thank you again to Julie, my editor, it's always an adventure working with you and I'm glad you're part of my team. Also, once again, thanks to the Tule team for working with me on this book.

Once again, this book was written alongside my bestie Abigail Owen. Your support gets me through the toughest days. And you never complain when I whine.

Jennifer, my tireless PA, another book completed with you working alongside me. Thanks for all your help and support.

To Shey and Shawn, still can't thank you enough for helping me out with my questions. And to their friend Jeff for sharing his experiences with me as I wrote this book.

Sometimes I need to tweak things a little for them to work in my world. Any inaccuracies or errors within the text are my own.

To my family, as always, I can't do half the stuff I do without knowing that I have your love and support fueling me to keep striving to reach my goals.

The Man's Best Friend series

Book 1: *Blind Date Bet*

Book 2: *Next Door Knight*

Book 3: Coming Soon

Available now at your favorite online retailer!

About the Author

USA Today Bestselling author Nicole Flockton writes sexy contemporary romances, seducing you one kiss at a time as you turn the pages. Nicole likes nothing better than taking characters and creating unique situations where they fight to find their true love.

On her first school report her teacher noted "Nicole likes to tell her own stories". It wasn't until after the birth of her first child and after having fun on a romance community forum that she finally decided to take the plunge and write a book. Now with over 20 books published she hasn't looked back.

Apart from writing Nicole is busy looking after her very own hero – her wonderfully supportive husband, and two fabulous kids. She also enjoys watching sports and, of course, reading.

Thank you for reading

Next Door Knight

If you enjoyed this book, you can find more from all our great authors at TulePublishing.com, or from your favorite online retailer.

TULE
PUBLISHING

Made in the USA
Columbia, SC
09 June 2019